THE CASTLE OF LOVE

The Earl was silent for a moment. "Who knows what will transpire," he murmured at last. He turned his head away and Jacina realised it was in an attempt to hide a grimace of pain.

Without thinking, she put her hand consolingly over his where it lay on the counterpane.

The Earl started at her touch. Then, slowly, his fingers closed over hers. He turned back to her, his features relaxing. She tried to draw her hand away, but he held it fast. Her heart began to pound as he raised her hand to his lips.

Jacina felt she would faint with the sensation that swept through her body. If only her hand could remain in his forever! His grasp was so strong! She felt herself drawn closer and closer.

"Forgive this display of weakness before a trusted friend," murmured the Earl.

A trusted friend! That was all she was to the Earl, all she would ever be.

Jacina closed her eyes. She reproached herself for imagining even for one second that she could be anything more.

The Barbara Cartland Pink Collection

Titles in this series

THE CASTLE OF LOVE

BARBARA CARTLAND

Barbaracartland.com Ltd

THE BARBARA CARTLAND PINK COLLECTION

Barbara Cartland was the most prolific bestselling author in the history of the world. She was frequently in the Guinness Book of Records for writing more books in a year than any other living author. In fact her most amazing literary feat was when her publishers asked for more Barbara Cartland romances, she doubled her output from 10 books a year to over 20 books a year, when she was 77.

She went on writing continuously at this rate for 20 years and wrote her last book at the age of 97, thus completing 400 books between the ages of 77 and 97.

Her publishers finally could not keep up with this phenomenal output, so at her death she left 160 unpublished manuscripts, something again that no other author has ever achieved.

Now the exciting news is that these 160 original unpublished Barbara Cartland books are ready for publication and they will be published by Barbaracartland.com exclusively on the internet, as the web is the best possible way to reach so many Barbara Cartland readers around the world.

The 160 books will be published monthly and will be numbered in sequence.

The series is called the Pink Collection as a tribute to Barbara Cartland whose favourite colour was pink and it became very much her trademark over the years.

The Barbara Cartland Pink Collection is published only on the internet. Log on to www.barbaracartland.com to find out how you can purchase the books monthly as they are published, and take out a subscription that will ensure that all subsequent editions are delivered to you by mail order to your home.

If you do not have access to a computer you can write for information about the Pink Collection to the following address :

Barbara Cartland.com Ltd.

240 High Road,

Harrow Weald,

Harrow HA3 7BB

United Kingdom.

Telephone & fax: +44 (0)20 8863 2520

THE LATE DAME BARBARA CARTLAND

Barbara Cartland who sadly died in May 2000 at the age of nearly 99 was the world's most famous romantic novelist who wrote 723 books in her lifetime with worldwide sales of over 1 billion copies and her books were translated into 36 different languages.

As well as romantic novels, she wrote historical biographies, 6 autobiographies, theatrical plays, books of advice on life, love, vitamins and cookery. She also found time to be a political speaker and television and radio personality.

She wrote her first book at the age of 21 and this was called Jigsaw. It became an immediate bestseller and sold 100,000 copies in hardback and was translated into 6 different languages. She wrote continuously throughout her life, writing bestsellers for an astonishing 76 years. Her books have always been immensely popular in the United States, where in 1976 her current books were at numbers 1 & 2 in the B. Dalton bestsellers list, a feat never achieved before or since by any author.

Barbara Cartland became a legend in her own lifetime and will be best remembered for her wonderful romantic novels, so loved by her millions of readers throughout the world.

Her books will always be treasured for their moral message, her pure and innocent heroines, her good looking and dashing heroes and above all her belief that the power of love is more important than anything else in everyone's life.

"Nothing in the world can ever equal love."

Barbara Cartland

CHAPTER ONE
1857

The *Star of India* was sailing towards the coast of England.

Hugo, Earl of Ruven stood alone on deck. He was enjoying the sound of the sails flapping in the breeze and the fresh, salty air. His cabin was comfortable but very small. In sultry weather such as they'd been having for the last few days, it became unbearably stuffy.

The sea breeze ruffled his thick, black hair.

Other passengers strolling along the deck, especially the ladies, turned to look at him as they passed.

He was a very handsome man. Tall and lean, his strong features were dark from his ten years in India. He had been an officer there with the Ninth regiment of foot.

Now he was sailing home to England.

The ladies longed to chat with him, but they learned that the Earl liked to keep himself to himself. He had spoken to hardly anyone during the entire voyage, taking his meals in his cabin and only venturing on deck when there were few other passengers about. Only his valet had been allowed to attend him.

"They say, Georgina, that we shall see the coast of England at any moment," said one of the ladies, ruefully eyeing the Earl's handsome figure as she sauntered by.

"That may be, Laetitia," replied her friend, "but let us hope the weather holds. I do not like the look of those dark clouds."

Laetitia lingered a moment and then turned back to the Earl. She was feeling a little more intrepid than usual today.

"Do you think, sir, there will be a storm before we reach England?" she asked.

The Earl did not even turn. He disliked the artificial tone of her voice. He had known so many ladies like her in India, officers' wives whose chief source of entertainment was gossip. "I am not an oracle, Madam," he said stiffly. "But the swell is certainly getting stronger."

"Well!" said Laetitia. She flounced off back to her companion. "Let us go to the other deck and find some *congenial* company!"

The Earl's lips tightened wryly but he kept his face turned towards the sea. The ship was beginning to pitch more steeply. Waves smacked loudly against the bows. He wondered if there would indeed be a storm before they reached England.

He leaned over the handrail and sighed.

His arrival in England would be a lonely one. His parents had died when he was a boy. They had been on a grand tour of Europe and had reached Naples when a typhoid epidemic broke out. They had succumbed to the disease within days of each other. Even as a boy Hugo had known that neither would have wanted to go on living without the other.

Hugo and his elder brother Crispian were at that time staying with their widowed grandfather, the old Earl, at Castle Ruven.

Crispian was now heir to the title.

The two boys, once they had recovered from the loss of their parents, enjoyed a happy childhood. Their grandfather was gruff but kind and indulgent. The boys slept in the nursery with their nanny Sarah. She would scold them mercilessly but they knew how to twist her round their little fingers.

The brothers had no other playmates but each other and consequently they were very close. They played hide and seek all over the castle and roamed the surrounding woods in the summer. Although he was the younger, Hugo was always the leader. Crispian was timid and introvert. It was Hugo who made him climb trees, swim in the swift flowing river, explore the local caves. When they were sent away to school, Hugo often had to protect the shy Crispian from bullies.

As the younger brother, Hugo needed a career. When the time came, his grandfather suggested the army. Hugo was happy with this idea. He was interested in travel, seeing the far-flung places of the world. So he became an officer with the Ninth regiment of foot and at twenty years of age set off for India.

It was the last time he saw his brother....

The Earl felt the ship rise steeply beneath him and then plummet into the waves. Spray lashed his face. There was a voice at his elbow. It was one of the crew. "Beg pardon, m'Lord. The Captain says you might think of coming below. Them clouds are nearly on us and the wind is getting up something fierce."

The Earl nodded. "Thank you. I will follow you down in a moment."

The crewman left. The Earl steadied himself on the rail and listened to the wind whistling through the masthead. The mournful sound seemed to echo his thoughts.

Why, when war broke out in the Crimea, had his usually timid brother insisted on doing his duty and joining the army? The old Earl was terribly reluctant to let his elder grandson go, but Crispian was for once very determined. In the end, and to his eternal regret, the old Earl agreed.

In January 1856, in the last months of the conflict, Crispian died of cholera. Hugo was heartbroken.

His grandfather wanted him home immediately but Hugo was not able to resign his commission until the following year. Then, shortly before he was due to leave, the Indian Mutiny broke out and Hugo was obliged to remain at his post.

Now the old Earl had died and Hugo had inherited the title and castle of Ruven.

He had also inherited Felice Delisle....

The Earl stiffened as he recognised unwelcome voices approaching. Laetitia and Georgina were returning, in the company of a young gentleman they had encountered on their tour of the decks.

Laetitia gave a shriek as the rising wind threatened to remove her bonnet from her head.

"Oh Lord," cried the young gentleman, "do hang on there! I do not fancy leaping into those waves to retrieve your bonnet, pretty as it is."

Laetitia laughed gaily and very loudly, partly for the benefit of the Earl. "Oh I should not expect it at all. But you are most courteous to even consider it, to be sure! And I do so admire courtesy in a man."

"Should we not go below now?" came Georgina's anxious voice. "That sailor said we should. And I am beginning to feel a trifle – queasy."

"Oh, if you wish," replied Laetitia. She threw a glance at the Earl. She was determined to impress him one way or another. "But I am not at all worried by the weather. I find it rather exciting!"

The Earl did not turn his head. He was too used to women who tried earnestly to attract his attention. There had, after all, been plenty of them, amongst the officers' daughters in India, and sometimes even amongst their wives.

"Is that not the Earl of Ruven at the handrail?" said the young gentleman.

"Yes it is," said Laetitia. She grabbed the young man's arm as the ship heaved into the face of a huge wave.

"Handsome fellow!" said the young man.

"Yes," said Laetitia sullenly. She was piqued at the Earl's evident disregard for her.

At that moment Georgina gave a great cry. "The coast of England! I am sure it is. There, to the north."

Georgina and her companions rushed to the bows for a sight of England.

The Earl lifted his head high. He appeared to be scanning the horizon. Nobody noticed the bitter smile on his lips.

He would have dearly liked to be able to catch a glimpse of his native country. But this was denied him.

In one of the early battles of the Indian Mutiny he had been seriously wounded.

Hugo, the handsome new Earl of Ruven, was returning home blind.

*

5

Castle Ruven was an imposing sight. It dominated the surrounding woods and crags that characterised the countryside of the far north of England. The castle was constructed of grey stone, much of it overgrown with ivy. A stone bridge arched over the surrounding moat. The bridge did not lead directly into the castle but into an area that had been cultivated as a garden. A white driveway ran over the bridge, through the garden and up to the wide entrance steps of the castle. Inside, the castle boasted a Great Hall with a minstrel's gallery.

The Great Hall was also the main entrance to the castle.

It was here that Doctor Carlton and his daughter Jacina stood a few days later, having just arrived at the castle in their pony and gig.

Jacina gazed round the Great Hall with admiration as she removed her bonnet. She loved the cool stone floor and the oak panelling, polished until it gleamed. She was fascinated by the family portraits that adorned the walls.

Jacina knew the castle well. She often accompanied her father on his visits here.

Her father was the Ruven family doctor. He had become a good friend of the old Earl and spent many an evening playing cards with him over a decanter of port. The old Earl had trusted the doctor so much, he had made him the executor of his will.

"Shall I take your hat too, Doctor Carlton?" asked the maid who had answered the door.

"Why, thank you, Nancy," said Doctor Carlton. "I expect you are all very busy here this morning! Is that why Jarrold did not answer the door as usual?"

Jarrold was the butler.

"Yes sir, that's why," replied Nancy. "The new Master

is expected around noon. Jarrold is upstairs overseeing the preparation of his private rooms. It was thought best to move some of the furniture out so it wouldn't be in the way. Seeing as the new Master is...is..."

Nancy could not go on and burst into tears.

"Now, now," said the doctor, patting her arm kindly.

"But it's all so dreadful, sir," wailed Nancy. "Poor Master Crispian dying out in the Crimea last year. Then the old Earl dying this February, with Master Hugo so far away. And then news that Master Hugo is...is..."

Nancy still could not bring herself to say the word 'blind.'

"Nancy," said Doctor Carlton, "you must keep up a cheerful spirit. It will not do for the new Earl to return to a gloomy household, will it?"

Nancy shook her head and sniffed away her tears, "No, sir." She took Jacina's bonnet and the doctor's hat and gloves. "Shall you go through to wait in the library, sir?"

"Indeed I shall. Would you order some tea for me?"

"Yes, sir. And Miss Jacina?"

"Thank you, not for me," said Jacina.

Nancy curtsied and hurried off. The doctor turned to his daughter. "I expect you are away on your usual social round, Jacina?"

"Yes, Papa."

"Good, good," said the doctor. "Well, you know where to find me."

Doctor Carlton went off in the direction of the library.

Jacina watched her father thoughtfully until he was out of sight. She knew he was more disturbed by what had happened to Hugo Ruven than he revealed.

Turning to go her eye settled on a particular portrait that hung over the stone fireplace. She went over and stood for a moment gazing up at it.

She knew this portrait well. It depicted the two grandsons of the old Earl, painted when they were in their late boyhood. Crispian was seated. Hugo leaned over the back of the chair. Crispian was pale and thin, with mournful eyes. Hugo gazed out forcefully from under his black brows. He looked strong and confident.

Jacina had met Hugo only once in her life. It was when she was eight years old and her father was attending the old Earl – who suffered from gout – for the very first time.

Jacina was sent to play outside. It was a blustery day. The wind tugged at her straw bonnet, as she ran down to the river that flowed through the castle grounds and into the moat. She watched in delight as a pair of white swans glided by with their cygnets.

Suddenly the wind snatched the bonnet from her head and sent it spinning into the swift flowing water. Jacina gave a cry. She ran alongside the river, keeping pace with her bonnet as it bobbed along. She did not know what to do except keep it in her sight.

She reached the point where the river swirled into the moat. The bonnet swirled with it. Once it entered the calmer moat waters, the bonnet remained almost at a standstill. Alas, it was still beyond her reach.

She looked round desperately. Perhaps she could find a branch, or a gardener's rake. Anything she could use to fish out her bonnet.

It was then she noticed a tall gentleman lounging against a nearby tree, watching her. He had dark eyes and a lock of black hair tumbled over his high forehead. Jacina could not help but notice the amused look on his face

"It's n..not funny," she said. Her red-gold hair glinted in the sun and her green eyes blazed with indignation.

The gentleman's expression immediately changed. "Indeed it is not," he said gravely, "and I humbly apologise for my frivolous demeanour. In recompense, will you allow me to retrieve your bonnet for you?"

Jacina looked at him doubtfully. "How will you retrieve it without a pole?" she asked. She looked back at the water and her lower lip began to tremble. "It's my v..very best bonnet, you know."

"Your very best!" exclaimed the gentleman. "Then there is no time to lose."

The gentleman removed his velvet jacket and pulled off his leather boots. Then, in his shirt and trousers, he jumped straight into the moat and waded out. Jacina was astonished.

The moat had silted up over the years and the water rose no higher than the gentleman's shoulders. He reached the bonnet without having to swim at all. When he returned to the bank, he vaulted up onto the grass. Then he bowed to Jacina.

"One very best bonnet," he said, holding it out.

The bonnet was soaked but Jacina clutched it to her as if it were a long lost treasure. "I do n..not know how to thank you, sir," she said.

"You can thank me by telling me your name."

"It is Jacina Carlton, sir."

"Ah! Your father is even now attending my grandfather, I believe?"

"Yes, sir."

The gentleman picked up his jacket and boots. " I

must return to the castle and change my clothes before supper." He gave another low bow. "Hugo Ruven, forever at your service."

With that he turned and disappeared among the trees.

Jacina saw no more of Hugo Ruven. Only two days later, he had sailed away to join his regiment in India.

That was ten years ago.

So much had changed for the worse for the Ruven family since then....

Jacina gave one last, sad glance at the portrait. Then she made her way to the castle kitchen. She liked to say hello to the cook, whom her father had often treated for what the cook called her 'bone troubles.'

The kitchen was in turmoil. Servants ran to and fro with platters on which sat the various dishes to be cooked for the new Earl's supper. There was a great side of ham and a huge salmon caught early that morning. There were pastries and pies and syllabubs.

The cook was pounding a slab of dough with her knuckles.

"Well, here's Miss Jacina," she said. Her face was red and shiny. She stopped to wipe her sleeve across her brow.

"You are working even harder than usual this morning," observed Jacina.

"That I am," said cook. "I'm making a rabbit pie for lunch. No decent pie without pain, that's the truth!"

"You are making a lot of things," said Jacina, looking round with wide eyes.

"I'm making things as'll have a nice, strong *smell*," said cook. "Because when a person can't see – " She didn't finish but shook her head sadly.

Jacina chatted for a little while and then said good-bye.

She left the kitchen and found the back stairs that led to the nursery. She was going to see old Sarah. Sarah had been nanny to Hugo and Crispian when they were boys. Jacina got to know her when her father came one winter to treat Sarah's chilblains.

The old nanny was sitting alone in the nursery. All about her were playthings from the childhood of her charges. There was a large white rocking horse. There was a wooden Noah's Ark complete with painted animals. There were books and balls and toy soldiers. Old Sarah kept the nursery just as it had been when Crispian and Hugo were boys.

She was always pleased to see Jacina.

She straightaway swung the kettle over the fire for tea. She could have rung down to the kitchen, but she knew they were busy. Besides, she was convinced she made better tea than anyone at Castle Ruven. She kept a caddy of her own in the nursery. The caddy was from India, with scenes of an exotic garden painted on it. Jacina often wondered if Hugo lived in a house with a garden like this around it.

Sarah fetched a biscuit jar from a cupboard and offered Jacina some shortbread while the tea brewed.

Jacina sat eating her biscuit while Sarah chatted about castle affairs.

"There's been such a bustle here since we heard the Earl was coming home. My poor master Hugo." Sarah wiped her eye with her apron. "Mercy me, what cruel times we've had."

Jacina brushed crumbs from her skirt and looked at Sarah thoughtfully.

"Sarah?"

"Yes, my lovely?"

"What will happen now to... Felice Delisle?"

"Bless me, don't you know the latest?"

Jacina shook her head. "I only really know what you tell me, Sarah. You know more than anyone."

This was true. Sarah knew everything that went on within the castle walls.

It was from Sarah that Jacina first heard the full story of Felice.

Felice was the daughter of Monsieur le Comte Delisle, an old friend of the Earl's, and a widower like himself. Monsieur le Comte had fled to Switzerland during the French revolution. He had lost his estates and so never returned to the country of his birth. He married late in life and still his young wife died before him. He became an inveterate gambler and died penniless, leaving his only child to the guardianship of the old Earl.

The old Earl did all he could for his ward. He settled a living allowance on her and made sure she went to a good school in Switzerland.

In the summer of 1852 the old Earl went travelling in Europe. He took his grandson Crispian with him. They stopped in Geneva, where Felice was at school, intending to stay for just a few days.

They ended up staying for over a month.

Felice was a pretty girl of sixteen. She had auburn hair and large eyes and was considered a very good pupil by Madame Gravalt, the owner and Headmistress of the school. It seemed inevitable that Felice and the shy heir to the Ruven title should fall in love. The Earl was secretly delighted but insisted they wait to be married. It was agreed that Felice should come to England to be married when she was twenty-one.

She never came.

In 1855 Crispian went to fight in the Crimea. He

wanted to prove to himself and his fiancée that he was brave. As brave as his younger brother Hugo.

He died shortly before the Crimean war ended.

Now the old Earl, Felice Delisle's guardian, was also dead.

Jacina thought it must be terrible to be an orphan and lose your fiancé and then your guardian. It was with all this in mind that she had asked Sarah what was to become of Felice.

"Well," said Sarah, peering into the teapot to see if the tea was brewed , "you know she took Master Crispian's death very hard and was ill in a sanatorium for a long time after?"

Jacina nodded.

"Well, after the illness, she went to live with this Madame Gravalt, who had meanwhile given up the school in Geneva and retired to a village in the mountains. I suppose she was as near to a family as Felice had. The old Earl invited Felice here but – " Sarah shook her head. "She didn't want to come. I suppose it were too soon to visit the place where Master Crispian grew up."

Sarah stopped to pour out two cups of tea. Jacina took her cup and dropped in some sugar. Sarah took a sip from her own cup and sat back with a sigh. Jacina waited, stirring her tea. She tried to be patient, but she found herself gradually stirring harder and harder, until the spoon tinkled loudly against the china. Sarah looked up, startled.

"What was I saying?" she asked.

"You were explaining why you thought Felice didn't accept the Earl's invitation to come and live here after Crispian died..." said Jacina, feeling a little ashamed of herself for having so startled the old lady.

"Ah yes." Sarah shook her head dolefully. 'The old Earl had grown very fond of her, you know. Not just for the sake of his friend, but also for her own sake. She was the daughter he never had. I'm sure that's why, after Master Crispian died, he started to encourage Master Hugo to take an interest in her."

Jacina felt herself go strangely still. "And did he...take an interest?"

"Well, he'd not met her, of course, but he started writing to her and she to him. During the whole year she was convalescing, they exchanged letters."

Sarah fell silent. Jacina waited. She could not understand why her heart seemed to be beating so quickly. She watched as the old nanny sighed and wiped her eyes with her apron.

"So they were writing to each other." Jacina prompted.

Sarah looked dazed for a moment. "Who, my lovely?"

"Felice and...Hugo."

"Oh, yes. Yes, they were. And some sort of understanding was growing between them, it seems. Because when the old Earl got ill, he asked Master Hugo to declare his intentions. So Master Hugo wrote back promising to marry Felice. The old Earl told me about it shortly before he died. It made him very happy."

Jacina drew in a deep breath before she spoke. "And *will* they marry, Sarah?"

Sarah frowned. "The talk now is that it won't happen. *'What young woman would want to yoke herself to an invalid'*, that's what they're all saying. But they're fools. Master Hugo is still a great catch. There's many a young lady of nobility round here wants him, if Miss Felice should change her mind. But she won't. Mark my words. The new Earl and Felice Delisle will marry here at Ruven before the year is out."

Before the year is out....

14

The blood rushed to Jacina's face and she looked away.

Why did the thought of Hugo Ruven getting married affect her so? After all, she had not had so much as a glimpse of him since that incident long ago when he rescued her bonnet.

From far below the open nursery window there came the sound of wheels on gravel. Jacina jumped up and ran to the sill. She leaned out to look.

Approaching the castle was a coach drawn by four white horses. Visible on the side of the coach as it swerved round the head of the driveway was the Ruven coat of arms.

The new Earl of Ruven was home.

CHAPTER TWO

Jacina hurried down the stairs. In the Great Hall, the servants were gathering to greet the new master of Castle Ruven. Jacina saw her father and went to his side. He glanced down at her and smiled but his eyes betrayed anxiety.

How would everyone respond to the sight of the blinded Earl?

The huge front door stood open. Jarrold the butler stood at the top of the flight of wide steps that led down to the driveway. He would be the first to greet the new Earl. He stood very upright as should befit his position.

The coach had drawn to a halt. The white horses pawed the ground and champed at the bit. They knew they were at the end of their journey and looked forward to mashed oats and the comfortable straw of their stables.

A footman, dressed in the Ruven colours of deep maroon and black, approached the coach. He pulled down the folding steps. Then he stood aside and with one smooth movement opened the coach door.

The first to step out was the Earl's valet. He turned at

the bottom of the folding steps and waited.

From within the coach, a hand appeared and grasped the frame of the door. With one swift movement, the Earl was out on the coach steps, straightened to his full height. So firm and unfaltering was his bearing, that those watching barely noticed him extend his right hand to the valet. The valet guided him down and then released his hand.

The Earl strode with head held high toward the castle steps.

Jacina's heart missed a beat. He was darker and leaner than when she had last seen him but the tilt of the head and the firm stride were the same.

The butler hastily descended the steps just as the Earl reached them.

"The first step, m'Lord," he whispered. For a moment, a frown crossed the Earl's forehead and the unseeing eyes seemed to darken. But he controlled whatever impatient thought was within.

"Thank you, Jarrold," he said. "It is Jarrold, isn't it?"

Jarrold bristled with importance. "Oh yes, indeed, m'Lord. It is Jarrold the butler here, sir. The household is in the Great Hall waiting to greet you, sir."

"Good. Then remind me, Jarrold. How many steps are here before me?"

"Just five, m'Lord."

"Thank you," said the Earl.

He ascended the steps without a stumble and passed into the Great Hall.

There was a stir amongst the waiting household. The mouths of the younger maids, those who had not been at the castle when Hugo was a young man, dropped open when they saw him. He was so tall and his shoulders so broad. His features were proud and even haughty, but he had the firm jaw of a man who kept his passions under control. His brow was dark and there was the hint of a sardonic twist to the full, red mouth.

His eyes were black and liquid. Their unseeing gaze was disconcerting.

Jacina thought how tired he must be after the long journey north, but he was most gracious as he moved along the line of waiting servants. Jarrold walked alongside him and told him whom he was meeting. The Earl inclined his head and spoke a few words to each person.

Cook had put on a clean apron. Her round, rosy face beamed as he asked if her cooking was as good as he remembered.

The Earl was coming to the end of the line of servants. He was very close now to Jacina. She could see the lines of fatigue on his face. She also saw for the first time a scar across his brow. This was surely from the injury that had blinded him.

Next to cook was Nancy. She impulsively put her hand out as the Earl approached, as if she wanted to touch him and be sure he was real. The Earl seemed to sense her hovering hand. He caught it in his own.

"Nancy, m'Lord," said Jarrold, with a frown at Nancy. She had overstepped the bounds.

"What, the little scold who used to help Sarah in the nursery, and scrub my head in the big tub by the fire?" asked the Earl with a lift of his brow.

"Oh yes, sir, that's me, sir," cried Nancy excitedly. The Earl had remembered her! "Only I'm not so little now, you wouldn't recognise me if you saw me..."

There was a barely audible gasp from the onlookers. Nancy's voice trailed off in dismay as she realised what she had said.

The Earl dropped her hand. Only Jacina noticed the faint flinch that crossed his features. "It must be borne," she heard him say under his breath. She knew it was meant for himself and not for Nancy.

Jarrold furiously motioned Nancy away. She scurried back to the kitchen, her apron over her head. Since Nancy had been at the end of the line, the other servants felt equally dismissed and started to hurry after her. They were eager to get out of earshot so they could discuss the events of the last few minutes.

"M'Lord," said Jarrold in a low voice, " I shall severely reprimand Nancy – "

"Jarrold," said the Earl wearily, "there are to be no repercussions."

Jacina understood what the Earl was thinking. There were likely to be many such blunders ahead of him.

Jarrold drew himself up. "Very well, m'Lord. And now, it remains for me to introduce you to Doctor Carlton and his daughter."

"Let me take your hand, Doctor Carlton," said the Earl. "We shall not stand on ceremony with each other. I have heard a great deal about you from my grandfather's letters. You were a conscientious doctor to him and a firm friend. I believe you even beat him at cards!"

"Not as often as he beat me," smiled the doctor. "He was a singular gentleman and I shall miss him greatly."

"I should like to talk more with you." said the Earl. "But first I wish to change out of my travelling attire.'

"We can return another time at your convenience," said the doctor.

"Oh no, I mean you to stay and take some refreshment

with me. If you do not mind waiting a little. I will change and then go and say hello to Sarah. She will be most displeased if I do not. But I shall not be long."

"We can wait in the library," said the doctor.

Jacina was standing by with downcast eyes. Jarrold had quite properly acknowledged her presence, but since that moment the Earl and her father seemed to have forgotten she was there. She was feeling rather as if she did not exist when she suddenly heard her name spoken.

"Allow me to present my daughter, Jacina," said the doctor.

Looking up, Jacina saw that the Earl had turned his head to the right of her father and not to the left where she actually stood.

"My Lord," she said quickly.

Earl Hugo turned his head in her direction. She dropped a curtsy. He might not be able to see it, but she knew he would hear the sweep of her muslin skirt on the stone floor. For a second, she fancied she saw his lip curl in a faint smile. She could not be sure, for a moment later he held his hand out for her to take and she felt the blood rush to her face. Hesitatingly, she placed her hand in his. It seemed to disappear in his strong grasp.

"Jacina," he murmured. "An unusual name. I do not believe I have heard it before."

"It was my mother's, my Lord," said Jacina, her heart flooded with disappointment. He had remembered the cook and he had remembered Nancy, but he had not in the least remembered her!

The Earl bowed over her hand and then turned back to her father.

"Let us meet in the library in half an hour," he said. "I trust you can entertain yourselves until then. What can I order for you?"

"We will wait until you join us," smiled the doctor.

Jarrold gestured to the valet, who had been waiting in the background all this while. The valet came forward. The Earl was tired now and grateful to put his hand on his valet's shoulder. His valet guided him to the foot of the grand stairway and the two figures ascended.

"Come, Jacina," said the doctor.

Together father and daughter walked to the library.

*

An hour later the doctor and the Earl were ensconced in deep wing chairs, drawn up on either side of a fire that was not lit. It was still only September and rather warm.

A maid had brought in tea and biscuits for Jacina. The Earl had ordered a rare bottle of Scotch whisky to be brought up from the cellar. He prevailed upon the doctor to partake of a glass with him.

"I should not," laughed the doctor. "I have rounds to finish."

"Surely you will join me in a toast to my grandfather?" coaxed the Earl wickedly.

"Ah, now that I cannot resist," said the doctor. He and the Earl lifted their glasses and drank.

Jacina sat on the window seat, her hands in her lap. She could feel the warmth of the sun on the nape of her neck. She knew the Earl could not see her and yet she was still too shy, too sensitive, to stare brazenly in his direction. The glances she cast him were surreptitious.

He had changed into a dark green velvet waistcoat and white silk shirt. One hand trailed over the side of the wing chair. The other nursed the crystal glass of whisky.

What a silly fool she was, she told herself. Why

should the Earl have remembered her? Even had he been able to see her, he could not possibly have recognised her. She had been a child of eight when he had encountered her and now she was a young woman of eighteen. Besides, for ten years he had been living a life of such adventure in India, that the mere rescuing of a bonnet would have paled into insignificance.

She, on the other hand, had remained here in the locale of Ruven, where over the years she had had plenty of opportunity to hear about Hugo and his exploits.

Hugo Ruven had been her childhood hero. No other young gallant in the neighbourhood had ever quite matched up. Since she was sixteen she had had a number of suitors but none of them interested her.

Her father laughed and called her a singular young lady.

The loss of her mother when she was ten had introduced a certain solemnity to her character. Helping her father at his surgery, accompanying him on his rounds and the hardships she had witnessed had taught her to curb her youthful wilfulness. She was neither a flirt nor had she a frivolous nature.

Yet she still had a sense of fun and she was very lovely to look at. The red gold tones of her hair were more muted but still lustrous. Her dazzling smile smote many a would-be suitor's heart.

None of this was of any consolation to her now that she was once again in the presence of Hugo Ruven.

What beauty she had was immaterial. He could not see it. Her smile, her green eyes, her translucent skin – inherited from her Highland mother – were wasted.

Even if he could see her, even if he did then admire her, what good would it do? She was a mere country doctor's daughter while he was an Earl.

He was also a man who was already engaged to be married.

Whenever Jacina pictured Felice Deslisle she pictured someone breathtakingly exotic. Felice was French. She was an orphan. She had spent her life abroad. She had endured the tragic loss of her first fiancé. She read deeply and obviously wrote such romantic letters that a man she had never met proposed to her. She was like the heroine of a novel!

Jacina sighed. She had no right at all to yearn after the Earl. All she could do was gaze on him from afar. This thought made her feel like a cat, hiding under a chair, gazing up at a king.

"Jacina, Jacina, are you dreaming?"

She started at the sound of her name. "I am sorry, Papa. The sun here at the window is making me sleepy."

"I was telling the Earl that you are my little helper," said the doctor.

"I am happy to be so," said Jacina simply.

The doctor turned back to the Earl. "Most young women would flinch at some of the sights we see on my rounds. Not my daughter!"

The Earl listened quietly. "You are lucky to have her."

"She sat with your grandfather a good many night, when Sarah was too tired, and I was not available."

"I am grateful indeed," said the Earl. He turned his glass slowly in his hand. "Tell me, did my grandfather suffer much at the end?"

"I am happy to tell you he did not. His heart just grew weaker and weaker. He was confined to bed for a month and died in his sleep." The doctor paused. "He was never the same after your brother's death. It was a mortal blow to him. He longed for your return."

"Alas, I could not resign my commission immediately," said the Earl. "There was a great deal of unrest in India. Lord Dalhousie had alienated many traditionalists with his reforms of ancient institutions."

Jacina was listening keenly. She now ventured a question. "Excuse me, Papa, but who was Lord Dalhousie?"

"He was Governor General of India," said the doctor.

The Earl had for the first time turned at the sound of Jacina's voice. Perhaps he was surprised that a provincial young lady should express an interest in the politics of the day.

Jacina's heart fluttered at the sight of the Earl's face turned towards her.

"Lord Dalhousie resigned in '56," Doctor Carlton mused. "Did matters not settle down then?"

The Earl turned back towards the doctor. "They did not. The rumble of discontent went on. Then in May this year the mutiny broke out. Mutineers from three regiments seized Delhi. It was late June before the British managed to capture one of the ridges overlooking the city."

There was silence for a moment. Then the doctor spoke. "It was at Delhi that you yourself were injured, I believe?" he said softly.

"It was," replied the Earl dryly. He took a sip of whisky from his glass. "The siege had barely begun. A cannon exploded beside me and shrapnel hit me on the forehead. When I regained consciousness, I was blind."

Jacina's eyes filled with tears as she listened.

"What prognosis have the experts given?" asked the doctor.

"The doctors in London said it might be what is called a 'trauma blindness.'"

Doctor Carlton nodded. "That occurred to me as soon as you described the accident. No doubt the experts explained that with an injury of this nature you may, in the fullness of time, regain your sight."

The Earl gave a dry laugh. "Of what practical use is that to me? When an expert says that I may regain my sight, he is equally saying that I may not! I refuse to live with false hope."

"Only you can decide what is the best way to deal with this affliction," said Doctor Carlton carefully.

"Affliction indeed!" said the Earl. He mused for a moment before continuing, "I am only grateful that my grandfather died before it happened."

"That was something of a blessing," said the doctor. "And, of course, he died happy with the knowledge that you intended to marry Felice Delisle."

"Ah, yes, Felice," said the Earl.

Jacina straightened at the sound of that name on his lips. She was longing to know what his thoughts were about the woman he was to marry. Was it possible to be in love with someone you had never actually met?

The Earl was ruminating. "The question is, though I may wish to marry Felice, will she now wish to marry me? I am not the man whose proposal she accepted. She does not know what has happened to me."

"I must interrupt there," said the doctor hurriedly. "She does know what has happened."

The Earl looked surprised. "How on earth – ! I had not yet informed her. I was uncertain as to how to break the news to her. I feared she might be in too delicate a state. She lost her first fiancé, my brother, as you know, and was ill for some time. She wrote to me after my grandfather died in February and sounded most desolate. I have not heard from her since. I was hoping to discuss the matter with someone who perhaps had some indication as to her current state of mind – someone like yourself – before I burdened her with further unpleasant news."

"I must apologise if I have exceeded my duties," said the doctor. "I wrote to her in June, as soon as I heard of your injury. I had already had occasion to write to her as executor of your grandfather's will."

The Earl, who had been brooding on the doctor's words, now gave a start. "She was a beneficiary, even though she was going to be married to me?"

"She was," said the doctor. "I was privy to your grandfather's thoughts on this subject. Perhaps you would like me to explain them?"

The Earl nodded. He reached forward and felt for the table at the side of his chair, where he carefully deposited his glass. Then he sat back to listen.

"Your grandfather was delighted when you wrote promising to marry Felice," said the doctor. "He was extremely fond of her and he wanted to make sure her future was utterly secure. The Ruven estate is entailed, remember. Should you marry Felice and then die before her and – God forbid – without issue, the whole estate would pass to a distant male relative. Since Felice has no family money of her own, she could in that case be left with very little. So your Grandfather arranged a generous sum to be settled on her in the unhappy event of your death. She would of course by law retain the title of Countess."

"I see," said the Earl.

"She sent a most courteous letter acknowledging mine in early March," said the doctor. "She was saddened by the old Earl's death and most touched by his thoughtfulness. I did not communicate with her again until June, when I sent her news of your injury."

The Earl interrupted with a bitter laugh. "And, knowing how things stand with me, she has not deigned to write to me since then!"

Jacina bowed her head. For the Earl to speak in such a tone meant only one thing. He was in love with Felice Delisle!

The doctor had also noted the Earl's reaction. "I did feel," he said gently, "that Miss Delisle should be informed of what had happened to you."

"Of course, of course," said the Earl. He had picked up his glass again and was tapping his fingers on the crystal.

"As to you not having heard from her," went on the doctor, "I should not take that as any indication of her state of mind concerning you. You have forgotten how difficult it was to get letters through during the mutiny."

"It was difficult indeed," agreed the Earl.

"I have a letter with me that should further reassure you," said the doctor. "Shall I read it to you?"

"By all means," said the Earl.

There was silence for a moment as the doctor patted his waistcoat pockets for the letter and his pince-nez. All Jacina could hear was the ticking of the large gilt clock that stood on the marble mantelpiece.

At breakfast some weeks before she had seen the letter with the foreign postmark but her father – such was his sense of propriety – had divulged nothing of its contents. Now she waited apprehensively while her father settled his pince-nez on his nose and began to read.

"Dear Doctor Carlton,

I write on behalf of my client, Mademoiselle Felice Delisle.

Mademoiselle Delisle wishes to thank you for your letter in June. She apologises for not replying sooner. She also apologises for not writing herself. She has been cast down with grief since hearing of the injuries to her fiancé Hugo. She understands that you are expecting him home by September at least. She wishes me to advise you that she intends to travel to England in November to be with him.

Her feelings for Earl Hugo are unchanged."

The doctor removed his pince-nez and looked at the Earl. "It is signed by a Monsieur Phillipe Fronard, notary at law," he said.

The Earl lifted his head. His features were impassive and his voice when he spoke betrayed nothing.

"It seems then that I am to have a wife after all."

"This surely calls for another toast!" said the doctor.

The Earl gave a quick smile. "Indeed." He turned his head towards where Jacina sat at the window. "Miss Carlton, will you join us?"

"I...I only have tea here, my Lord."

"I am sure tea will prove equal to the task," said the Earl.

With a trembling hand, Jacina lifted her china teacup from its tray.

"To my future wife, Felice Delisle," said the Earl.

"To your wife," echoed the doctor.

"To your wife," said Jacina in a low voice.

She took a sip of tea. It was cold. She put down her cup and turned her face to the window. Her eyes were misty and she fiercely blinked away the incipient tears. She was cross with herself for being so affected. She was not one of those girls who had nothing but romance and embroidery to occupy their minds! She was luckier than most. Her father often allowed her to be involved in his work. She had the opportunity to make herself truly useful.

Jacina Carlton, you are not to be a silly fool, she told herself.

She heard the Earl rise and make his excuses. He had other castle business to attend to.

"As do I," smiled the doctor. "Some of the families on the Ruven estate are also my patients."

"We have much to discuss on other occasions," said the Earl.

Jarrold escorted the doctor and his daughter to the entrance, where their gig had been brought round to the bottom of the steps.

Jacina was very quiet as she and her father drove home. She turned her head only once, to catch a last glimpse of the castle. It looked so imposing on its ridge above the trees.

A disturbing thought crossed her mind as she looked back.

It would be better for her if she never saw the castle or the Earl again!

CHAPTER THREE

A week later Jacina and her father sat at breakfast in their little parlour.

At the doctor's elbow was a pile of books. Doctor Carlton was interested in epidemiology and, to Jacina's amusement, often had his head in a book all through breakfast.

This morning however the books remained closed. The doctor coughed and regarded Jacina over the top of his pince nez.

"Jacina."

"Yes, Papa?"

"I have found employment for you."

She looked at him quizzically. "Yes, Papa?"

"It is connected with the Earl."

Jacina toyed with her teaspoon. "Oh?"

Her father had been twice to sup at the castle, but each time Jacina had declined the invitation, pleading a headache.

"He is a proud man and does not like to accept help,"

explained the doctor, "but even he has to admit that the one thing he cannot do for himself is read the newspapers. Yesterday he asked whether I knew of anyone who might come to the castle and read to him. Without a second thought I suggested you ."

"Oh Papa," burst out Jacina, "I wish you had not!"

The doctor looked astonished. "Why Jacina, what possible reason could you have to refuse?"

Jacina stared into her cup. She had resolved not to return to Castle Ruven until she believed herself to be immune to the Earl's attractions, but she did not feel she could tell her father this.

"S..surely his steward and secretary are more equal to the task?" she murmured instead.

"His steward and his secretary read official papers but he says that is quite enough. He finds their voices grating. You are the perfect candidate. The Earl himself reflected that you have a sweet tone of voice. He was also impressed that you seemed to take an interest in the world at large."

"But Papa, I like to go with you on your rounds!"

"The Earl would only require your help each morning," said the doctor. "That would still leave the afternoon for you to accompany me." The doctor regarded his daughter closely. "I do not understand your reluctance. You would have access to all those books in the Earl's library. And Sarah was delighted when I told her you might be at the castle every day."

At this mention of Sarah, Jacina fell silent.

*

The very next day the Ruven coach was once more making its way up the long driveway to the castle. The white coats of the horses shone in the newly risen sun.

The Earl had sent the coach early to collect Jacina. Her father's mention of Sarah had undone her resolution not to return to Castle Ruven, until she was resistant to the Earl's charms. She gazed out at the frosty woods, hugging her green cloak tight about her.

Jarrold was waiting on the castle steps. He came down and opened the coach door. "His Lordship is in the library," he told her.

The Earl sat in the wing chair before the fire, just as he had done on her last visit. This time the fire was lit. The Earl looked very distinguished in black. He turned his head towards the door as it opened. With a pang Jacina saw that his features were drawn and weary, as if he had not slept well.

"Miss Jacina Carlton, m'Lord," announced Jarrold.

Jacina stood uncertainly in the doorway.

"Well, step forward," said the Earl.

She went forward and took his outstretched hand. His fingers closed tightly over hers. "A cold hand!" he exclaimed. "Were you not wearing gloves?"

"I forgot them, my Lord," said Jacina.

She could not tell him how flustered she had been that morning, preparing to leave for the castle. Neighbours had stood on their doorsteps, watching with interest as she had entered the grand coach marked with the Ruven coat of arms.

"Well, come and sit down," said the Earl. "I told Jarrold to manoeuvre your chair so that you get light from the window to read by as well as sufficient warmth from the fire. I hope it is placed to your satisfaction?"

"Thank you...yes...it is," said Jacina.

She sat down opposite the Earl. By her chair stood a small table on which was placed a newspaper. The Earl asked whether she wanted some tea but she said she would wait.

"You have, I hope, conquered your ill health?" enquired the Earl politely.

"My...ill health?" repeated Jacina.

The Earl raised an eyebrow. "The headaches that deprived us of your company at supper on at least two occasions this week," he said.

Jacina bowed her head against his unseeing gaze. "I am much improved...my Lord," she murmured.

"That is good," said the Earl. He turned his face towards the fire and fell silent. Jacina waited.

"My Lord," she began after a moment or two.

The Earl lifted his head. "Yes?"

"Shall I...begin reading?"

"Of course, of course." He gestured in the direction of a small table on which the newspaper waited.

Jacina took up the newspaper and began reading the main article. It was concerned with the situation in India and described the endeavours of the British to retake positions that had fallen to the rebels.

Every so often Jacina paused and stole a glance at the Earl. He had rested an elbow on an arm of the chair and leaned his head on his palm. A lock of his dark hair fell forward. Suddenly he gave a loud groan.

"Enough!" he cried. "Why should I listen to this? What has any of it to do with me now?"

Jacina listened in dismay. "But...my Lord...one must know...what is happening in the world."

"Oh, must one?" said the Earl. The unexpected coldness in his voice made Jacina tremble but she stood firm.

"It is easy to...retreat from the world...then you... retreat from people and then...in the end...from your very self."

The Earl's lips curled. "You speak with such authority for one so young."

Jacina lifted her head. "I have witnessed it, my Lord. In my father's patients...there are those who endure and those who..." She bowed her head again, unable to continue.

"And those who capitulate!" the Earl finished for her. "Is that what you were about to say?"

"Yes," said Jacina miserably.

The Earl's dark, unseeing eyes seemed to glaze over. He sank back in his chair. "It must be borne," he murmured.

There was silence between them. Logs in the fire snapped and the clock ticked on. Jacina's eyes roved desperately over the room. In the far corner she noticed a small pianoforte. It was not as grand as the pianoforte that she knew stood upstairs in the music room, but it was a perfectly adequate instrument.

"Shall I play for you, my Lord?" she asked.

The Earl made a desultory gesture. "Why not?"

Jacina rose and crossed to the pianoforte. She raised the lid and sat down. She thought for a moment and then began to play a soothing piece from memory. After a moment she completely lost herself in the melody and began to sing.

The sound seemed to sweeten the very air in the room.

When she had finished playing she looked over to where the Earl was sitting. As if sensing her gaze, he turned towards her. His features had softened. "Come here, Jacina," he said.

She closed the lid and rejoined him at the fire.

The Earl bent his head for a moment before speaking. "I believe I have misused you this morning," he said. "I humbly apologise."

Looking at him, Jacina saw again the proud young man who had apologised for laughing at her when she lost her bonnet.

"Your dulcet tones when reading made me relax my guard," went on the Earl. "I gave vent to feelings that had become insupportable. It will not happen again. I have no wish to scare you off so soon. I have a feeling your company is going to be as good for me as one of your father's tonics. Will you forgive me? Will you promise to continue to be my little helper?"

Jacina's thoughts were swimming.

It was torture for her to be near the Earl and know she could never allow herself to feel more for him than friendship. Yet how she could resist his plea that her company would do him good?

"I shall be happy to...continue to be...of service, my Lord," she ventured at last.

The Earl smiled. " Then let us shake hands on it, Jacina Carlton!"

With that, he leaned forward and folded her hand firmly in his.

*

The weeks that followed were unexpectedly happy for Jacina. Morning after morning, she had the Earl to herself. The Earl listened quietly as Jacina read the newspapers to him. Sometimes they discussed the contents. The Earl was charmed at Jacina's curiosity about the world. Soon he was asking her to choose something to read from the great collection of books in the library. He began to take great pleasure in discussing his favourite authors with her.

She often played the pianoforte for him and sometimes she sang. The Earl would listen with lowered head, his hand across his eyes. Jacina's sweet voice touched his soul and he felt the horror of what he had experienced in India begin to melt away.

Jacina never allowed a single untoward thought about the Earl intrude into her mind. It was enough for her to just be with him. She ceased to think about how this idyll might end.

When the weather was mild the Earl and Jacina took to strolling in the castle grounds together. The Earl had so far relaxed with his little helper, that he would lean lightly on her arm whenever he felt unsure of the terrain.

Jacina had often wandered through the castle grounds, while her father attended the old Earl or the cook or Sarah. She led the Earl along paths that even he had forgotten from his youth.

She became his eyes, describing the giant elms and oaks, the changing colours of their leaves. She described the mist on the highest mountain crags and the shapes of clouds.

One day they found themselves on the bank of the river.

Falteringly, Jacina described the sun glinting on the water and on the snowy plumes of the swans. She could not bring herself to ask the Earl whether he remembered the bonnet bobbing along on the river's surface all those years ago. The Earl noticed the tremor in her voice. "What is here that you do not wish to describe to me?" he asked.

"N..nothing, my Lord," cried Jacina.

"You must not hide anything unpleasant from me," the Earl said. "Do you see the carcase of some animal or the feathers of a bird? Is there evidence of poaching?"

"There is not, my Lord."

"Then what is it that is so affects you?" the Earl persisted.

Jacina hung her head. "It is just...I see...something... from the past.'

"Something from the past?"

"On the river."

The Earl looked bemused. "What is it?"

"A...b..bonnet, my Lord."

There, thought Jacina. It is out. Now he can laugh at me for remembering it so clearly all these years.

The Earl did not laugh, though a faint smile touched his lips. "A bonnet?" he repeated. "A bonnet with a blue ribbon that trailed in the water behind it? A *very best bonnet*?"

Jacina gasped. "You...remember...my Lord?"

"I remember the incident and the spirited little girl," said the Earl. "What a fool I am for not remembering her name, or that she was the doctor's daughter! Please forgive me. So much has happened in the years since to erase even the most pleasant memory." He paused and then reached for her. Taking her gently by the shoulders he turned her to him as if he was able to look at her face. His eyes, blind though they were, seemed to burn into hers. She found herself lowering her gaze.

"Now my mind can put a face to your voice," he murmured.

"I am much...changed...my Lord," said Jacina.

"What?" laughed the Earl. "You do not still have green eyes and golden hair with a hint of red?"

"I..I do, my Lord. But I was a child then. I am a..a woman now."

The Earl dropped his hands from her shoulders as suddenly as if they had been scalded. "Of course," he said. "You are a woman now. Come, let us turn back."

The swans amid the reeds watched as Jacina led the Earl away.

The weather changed the very next morning. The horses bringing Jacina to the castle splashed through great puddles. Jarrold rushed out with an umbrella to hold over her as she ascended the castle steps.

The newspaper that morning reported an outbreak of cholera in the city of Edinburgh. The Earl was troubled. His own parents had died of typhoid when he was a boy and he had since witnessed the ravages of such diseases in India.

"We have not been exposed to either typhoid or cholera here at Ruvensford within my memory," Jacina told him.

"Long may it remain so," said the Earl.

He asked Jacina about the local families, those who were tenants on his land.

Jacina knew many of them from accompanying her father on his rounds. She described their lives and their troubles to the Earl. He was struck by her compassion for those less fortunate than herself.

The Earl gradually began to confide more and more in Jacina.

He never talked about his experience of the mutiny, but he described other aspects of his life in India. She enjoyed hearing about the landscape and the customs of the people.

"The men are dark and handsome," he said. "The women wear bright colours and are like exotic birds."

Jacina felt a pang of jealousy. The Earl had admired the beauty of those women in a way that he would never, could never, admire Jacina.

She wondered about the English women attached to the regiment.

As if he read her thoughts, the Earl continued. "Mostly we mixed only with the wives and daughters and sisters of the regiment. They were our partners at balls and suppers. I myself led a rather solitary life there. Particularly after I became engaged to Felice."

The Earl's admission of fidelity to a woman he barely knew – and that only by letter – disturbed Jacina. Felice must have some strange power over men to have so affected the Earl.

It was a power that she, Jacina, could never imagine possessing.

*

Doctor Carlton had become very preoccupied of late, particularly since receiving a letter from his friend who was a professor of epidemiology at Edinburgh. When not visiting his patients he shut himself away in his study, scrutinising his medical tomes. He no longer visited the Earl for supper or to play cards.

Jacina was surprised when one morning her father put on his cloak and joined her in the coach that had arrived to take her to the castle.

"I need to speak to the Earl," was all he would tell his daughter.

There was a log fire blazing merrily in the library when they entered. The Earl was astonished when he realised that the doctor had arrived with Jacina. He politely motioned them to be seated.

"You must excuse my intruding on your morning like this," said the doctor. "But dire necessity has driven me here."

Jacina rose. "Do you wish to speak to the Earl alone, Papa?"

"No, no," said the doctor. "What I have to say concerns you."

"Me, Papa?" Jacina sat down again in some alarm.

Doctor Carlton wiped his brow with a handkerchief. "No doubt you have heard of the recent outbreak of cholera in Edinburgh?" he said to the Earl.

"I have," said the Earl. "I took comfort in the fact that it was far over the border."

"Oh, I have no fears of it spreading south," said the doctor. "I am, however, very interested in such diseases. My old professor at Edinburgh University has written to me. He would be grateful for my help in controlling this outbreak and I am very inclined to go. My only concern is Jacina."

"But Papa," cried Jacina. "I must go with you!"

Despite her pleasure in being with the Earl, she was convinced that her duty lay in helping her father. A strange look crossed the Earl's features, as he heard her words and he turned his face to the fire for a moment.

Doctor Carlton was shaking his head at his daughter. "No, Jacina, I could not expose you to such a danger."

"But Papa..."

The doctor was firm. "You will not change my mind about this," he said. "I do not wish you to accompany me and equally I do not wish you to remain at home alone."

The Earl turned back from the fire to listen.

The doctor continued. "My purpose in coming to the castle this morning is to request that the Earl take you under his full protection during my absence."

"Do you mean me to...to stay here...at the castle?" stammered Jacina." If the Earl so agrees," said her father.

The Earl almost leapt to his feet. "I do indeed agree. It is a capital idea. I – that is Sarah – will be delighted to have more of your daughter's company."

Jacina looked away. She could not hide her disappointment that the Earl had said it was *Sarah* who would be delighted, not he.

The doctor and the Earl shook hands.

"Rest assured, we will all endeavour to make your daughter feel at home here," smiled the Earl.

"I am eternally grateful for your help," said the doctor.

Thus it was settled that Jacina became a permanent guest at Castle Ruven for the duration of her father's absence in Edinburgh. She was desolate saying good-bye to her father. She worried for his safety and at first she missed him terribly. At the same time she could not help but be delighted with her new life at the castle.

Her bedchamber was in one of the towers. The bed was a four-poster, hung with rose coloured silk. She had never slept in such luxury nor been so indulged. Every morning Nancy would come in to light the fire and draw the curtains before bringing Jacina a tray of hot chocolate and buttery biscuits. While Jacina ate her breakfast Nancy would bring in jugs of hot water to fill the bath, which stood in the corner of the chamber behind an ivory screen.

"Nancy, you are making me feel guilty," laughed Jacina.

"You enjoy it, miss," said Nancy. "It won't last forever."

Jacina spent every morning with the Earl as usual. In the afternoons she read in her chamber or continued the studies that her father had begun with her in French and Latin. Sometimes she would go to the nursery, where Sarah would make tea and gossip. If the weather was fine she would put on her cloak and set out to visit poor families on the estate. She would take them provisions, which cook was always happy to make up for her in a little basket.

The Earl dined alone unless he had guests. Then Jacina was invited to join him. The Earl and his guests discussed estate business or politics. Jacina was happy to listen and gaze about her at the ornate dining hall.

If she did not join the Earl she took supper in her room, or with Sarah. Afterwards she would wander the long corridors looking at all the paintings. She had to pinch herself to think she was actually a guest in the castle she had admired for so long.

One morning, the Earl asked Jacina if she would like to see those parts of the castle that had been shut up since before the old Earl died. Jacina was intrigued and said she would.

A little while later her heart fluttered with anticipation as a huge oak door creaked slowly open onto a long gallery.

The day had turned windy and storm clouds were gathering over the crags. Boughs lashed the mullioned windows as the Earl and Jacina strolled along. Portraits of early ancestors hung on the gallery walls.

Jacina stopped in front of a painting of a beautiful young woman. "Who is that, my Lord?" she asked.

"You must describe her to me before I can answer," the Earl gently reminded her.

Jacina blushed at her mistake. She described the painting. The woman had huge eyes and raven tresses. She wore a magenta gown and a diamond necklace glittered around her white neck.

The Earl nodded. "Ah, yes. That is my grandmother. Her private chambers occupied this part of the castle. After she died my grandfather could not bear to come here and had it all closed up. But yesterday I ordered it reopened."

Jacina sighed as she gazed at the painting. "She is

so...so lovely. Her dress is such a beautiful colour. And the necklace..."

The Earl looked thoughtful. "Would you like to see that necklace?" he asked.

Jacina's eyes grew wide. "You...still have it, my Lord?"

The Earl laughed. "It is a family heirloom. Come with me, Jacina."

Such was his memory of the castle's layout, that it was with no difficulty he led Jacina to the end of the gallery and thence into a corridor that ran to the north east tower.

As if by instinct he stopped outside a door that opened from the corridor into a large and opulent room. The walls of the room were hung with yellow silk. The four poster bed was of carved oak . The mirrors on the walls were framed in gold. A walnut dressing table stood by the window.

The Earl let his fingers roam over the dressing table until they found a blue leather jewellery case. He opened it and Jacina gasped.

There, on a purple velvet cloth, lay the necklace she had seen in the painting.

"Try it on," suggested the Earl.

With trembling hands Jacina draped the necklace around her neck and fastened the clasp. She stood back and gazed at her reflection in the dressing table mirror.

"How do they look?" asked the Earl.

"They...they dazzle..." she replied in a low voice.

She wished that the Earl could see her. She looked very becoming in the necklace.

The Earl sighed behind her. "It is family tradition that they are handed on through each generation to the eldest son's bride" he said.

Jacina understood in a flash. This part of the castle

had been re-opened for Felice. This room was being prepared for Felice. And this necklace, this string of diamonds and rubies that dazzled her in the mirror, was also for Felice. With trembling fingers, Jacina tore it from her neck and threw it into the box.

"Please...I wish to...return to my room now, my Lord," she said.

The Earl had heard the sound of the necklace dropped rudely into the box and was puzzled. "What is the matter?" he asked gently.

"N..nothing. I...do not feel well, suddenly. That is all."

The Earl hesitated and then gave a small bow. "As you wish," he said.

In her room Jacina threw herself into a chair by the fire and stared miserably into the flames.

The more time she spent with the Earl, the more she resented the mere idea of Felice Delisle. Yet she knew this was unjust. It was not the fault of Felice that she had accepted the Earl's proposal. Felice had already suffered so much in her life, why should she not grasp at any opportunity of being happy?

The wind rattled the windows and sent smoke back down the chimney. Jacina drew her legs up under her and rested her chin on her knees. She reminded herself sternly that the Earl needed her. He enjoyed her company. She must be content with that for as long as it lasted and no more.

The following morning her mood had improved and so had the weather. By noon the sun had so warmed the air, that the Earl suggested Jacina read to him out of doors. They sat on a wrought iron bench placed in the shade of the castle wall. The Earl asked Jacina to read some poetry.

The sun was warm on Jacina's face. She turned the pages and read in a dreamy voice.

Suddenly the Earl raised his head. "What was that?" he asked.

"My Lord?"

"I heard the sound of coach wheels."

Jacina listened. Now she heard it too. A moment later a coach swept out of the line of trees on the other side of the moat and clattered over the stone bridge.

The Earl rose to his feet as the coach drew up at the castle steps. Jacina also rose, her heart full of foreboding.

A footman hurried out of the castle to open the coach door. First a gentleman in a cloak stepped out. He threw a sharp glance round him before turning to help out a second traveller.

This was a tall woman in a scarlet jacket. A veil was drawn down over her features, but Jacina had no doubt who it was. Felice Delisle!

The bride-to-be had finally arrived at Castle Ruven.

Jacina knew her idyll was over.

CHAPTER FOUR

Felice Delisle raised her veil and her eyes fell at once on Jacina. Her gaze was so cool and appraising that Jacina stepped back in surprise. She would never have guessed from this expression that here was a young woman about to meet her husband to be for the very first time.

She had to admit though that Felice was very handsome. Her auburn hair was arranged in the very latest fashion. Her eyes were large and the colour of amber. Her heart shaped face was fuller than Jacina had imagined, but then Felice was no longer the girl of sixteen with whom Crispian Ruven had fallen in love. She was now an elegant young woman of twenty-one.

Felice turned her cool gaze from Jacina to the Earl. "You are Hugo, I think!" she said in a low voice.

The Earl bowed and Felice extended her hand. The Earl seemed to sense her gesture. With barely a falter he took her hand and lifted it to his lips.

"Welcome to Castle Ruven," he said, in a most solicitous tone. "I hope your journey was not too tiring."

"It was terible, zis journey," said Felice with a shrug. "But anyhow, we are arrived." She gestured toward her travelling companion, seemingly unconcerned that the Earl could not register such a gesture. " Zis is my – how do you say it in England? – lawyer, yes? Monsieur Fronard."

"At your service," said Monsieur Fronard with a bow. He had a long, sharp face and a piercing gaze.

Felice's eyes flicked back to Jacina. "And who is zis person?" she asked.

"I am Jacina Carlton, Madame," said Jacina, curtseying.

The Earl smiled . "Ah, yes. Miss Carlton is my little helper."

"Zat's nice," said Felice. "And in what does she help you?"

"Mostly Miss Carlton reads to me, Madame."

"Oh," said Felice with a toss of her head. "Reading!" She said nothing more but took the Earl's arm. The two of them started up the stone stairway to the castle entrance.

Jacina followed. Monsieur Fronard fell quickly into step beside her. "You are an old friend of the Earl, no?" he asked her.

"My father has been the family doctor for many years," replied Jacina.

"Ah, je comprends," said Monsieur Fronard.

Quite what Monsieur Fronard 'understood' from her simple remark Jacina could not tell.

Over the next few days the atmosphere in the castle began to change. It no longer seemed so peaceful or indeed so sleepy. There was a great more scurrying to and fro in response to the imperious demands of the Earl's fiancée.

Her handkerchiefs must be pressed just so. The fire in

her room must be always lit. She must have hot water brought for a bath twice a day. Two maids must scrub her back and help her into her clothes. She must have champagne brought to her mid-morning.

She seemed determined to forget the privations she had once endured as the daughter of a penniless count and as a pupil in a strict teaching establishment. Day and night her gay laughter resounded through the castle and it was generally observed that the Earl must be enchanted with her.

Monsieur Fronard meanwhile set everybody's teeth on edge. He seemed to skulk about the place. The maids kept coming across him in out of the way places.

"I reckon he's counting the china, Miss Jacina," said Nancy indignantly one morning.

Jacina looked up from her bowl of porridge. She no longer took breakfast in her room, as she felt the maids had enough to do with running around after Felice.

"And I wish he hadn't been given Master Crispian's old room," Nancy went on. "It don't seem right, somehow. One morning I went in with clean linen and *she* was in there with him. They were burning letters in the grate. I was sure they were all the letters she wrote Master Crispian. He'd kept them in a box on his desk. Sure enough, when I looked in the box later, it was empty."

"She wants to make a fresh start," said cook stoutly, "and who can blame her?"

Nancy sniffed. "Well, I think she's heartless. And what's more, she's too fancy. Ordering all that French stuff from Fortnum's in London like – like truffles and – and caviar."

"She has sophisticated tastes, that's all." said cook. "Which his Lordship is only too happy to indulge. So what business is it of ours?"

Jacina listened with bowed head.

She had noticed that the Earl did indeed indulge every whim his fiancée expressed. He was courtesy itself with Felice.

Was Jacina the only one who felt Felice was less than courteous in return? She seemed almost impatient with the Earl's blindness. Walking through the corridors and galleries of the castle with him, she rarely allowed him to lean on her arm. She would move swiftly ahead to look at something and then wait, tapping her foot or sighing. At supper she sat next to the Earl, but never helped him if he happened to drop his napkin or misplace his glass. She always waited for one of the serving maids to come forward to retrieve the napkin from the floor or put his glass within his reach.

She was happy enough to drive out with the Earl and visit the local gentry, but she would never accompany him on his walks in the garden. Her excuse was that she did not like to walk in the countryside where there were no shops to look at or other people to meet. Jacina wondered that she did not find the Earl's company sufficient.

At table Felice sat between the Earl and Monsieur Fronard. Jacina noticed how Felice's head was turned most often toward Fronard. The Earl sat quietly by, listening to their conversation, which was in French. Sometimes he made a remark and Felice would turn quickly to him. She would laugh brightly, take up his hand and press it to her cheek. Then just as quickly, she turned back to Fronard.

Jacina wondered why Felice did not make more effort to talk with her fiancé. After all, they had so much ground to make up. It was true that Felice and her lawyer had a language in common. Yet the Earl spoke French and Felice had a good enough grasp of English for them to be able to communicate easily.

When Jacina thought about it, the person she saw most

often with Felice was Fronard. Even if the Earl happened to be present, the two of them would often be tucked away in some corner, heads together. Jacina often came upon them side by side in the corridors of the castle, looking at the portraits or the china in the cabinets. She began to get the distinct impression they were discussing the value of everything they looked at.

She wanted to like Felice, for the sake of the Earl. She tried to make friends with her, but Felice had decided that Jacina was merely another employee and rarely addressed her. As if in deference to the sensibilities of his fiancée, the Earl in public adopted a more formal manner with Jacina. This would have made her unutterably miserable were it not for the fact that during their mornings together, he continued to treat her in the old manner. She was relieved that in this respect everything went on as before. Jacina read or played the pianoforte. She and the Earl talked about poetry and music. They sometimes strolled in the garden.

They never discussed Felice or the forthcoming wedding.

One day, walking on the woodland path, the Earl's arm resting on Jacina's, they happened to encounter Monsieur Fronard. He greeted them politely but his eyes narrowed as they passed on.

The following morning when Jacina entered the library, she was startled to find Felice seated opposite the Earl at the fire.

"I hope you are not objecting," cried Felice gaily to Jacina, "but I am thinking my English will improve if I am listening to you."

"I am sure Jacina does not object," said the Earl. The tone of his voice was neutral.

"Of course not," said Jacina as brightly as she could. She hesitated, looking around. Then she went and sat in the window seat. She opened the book that the Earl had chosen for that day and began to read.

After about five minutes she heard Felice yawn loudly.

The Earl leaned forward. "You are tired, my dear?"

"Oh no," laughed Felice. "But zis book is not interesting to me."

Jacina closed the book quietly. "Perhaps something else?" she suggested. "There must be something. I know you love books."

Felice threw her a sharp glance. "Books? Oh yes. I am always reading. But zis book you have is not in my language, so it is difficult. And besides, history – " she shrugged. "I prefer – love stories. Tragic love stories – "

Words tumbled out of Jacina before she could stop herself. "I'm surprised you like such reading matter when you yourself have experienced..."

"Jacina!" said the Earl sharply.

Jacina's hand flew to her mouth. "My Lord, I wasn't thinking..."

"No," said the Earl, a thunderous look on his face. "You most certainly were not."

Unable to speak, Jacina stumbled to her feet and fled from the room.

What had possessed her to say what she did? If Felice enjoyed reading novels that could only remind her of the sad loss she had endured, well then...it was no business of Jacina's to comment. But the Earl had not been fair. He really had not. It was rude of Felice to yawn loudly! And what had the Earl done when he heard it? Nothing! Nothing but express concern that she might be tired!

It was clear that he was falling more and more deeply under Felice's spell.

Jacina sank on to a seat in the Great Hall and covered her face with her hands. Why should a man not fall under the spell of the woman who was to be his wife? It was only natural. She had no right to feel like this, no right at all.

Tears pricked her eyelids. She wished her father would return and take her away from the castle, but she knew that was impossible at the moment. Her father had written to say that the epidemic in Edinburgh was still raging and now his friend the professor was ill. Jacina could not possibly write and worry him with her selfish concerns.

Suddenly she felt that she was no longer alone. She took her hands away from her face and looked up.

Monsieur Fronard was leaning against the wall opposite, arms folded. His eyes regarded her narrowly.

"Something is ze matter?" he asked.

She shook her head. "No. That is...yes. I...I am worried about my father. And I'm...homesick. That is all."

"That is all?" Monsieur Fronard's tone was mocking. "Well, I think not. I think I know what is ze matter. How do you say it – your 'nose is out of place'."

Jacina rose trembling to her feet. "The phrase is 'out of joint'," she said as coldly as she could muster. "And now, if you'll excuse me, I must go to my room."

As she tried to pass, Fronard caught at her arm and held her.

"Nothing will threaten zis marriage, you understand," he scowled. "Nothing."

Jacina twisted in his grip. "Take your hand off me! What makes you speak to me like this?"

Fronard leaned close to Jacina and hissed in her ear. "I know what is in your heart. I am only warning you. Stay away from ze Earl. He is now only for Felice."

Jacina wrenched herself free. "I care nothing for the Earl," she cried, and turned on her heels.

Fronard's jeering laugh followed her. "You are lying, Mademoiselle. You are lying!"

His words rang in her ears. How could he know 'what was in her heart' when she hardly knew herself? What did his warning mean? In what way could her friendship with the Earl threaten the marriage? Everyone knew that the Earl was enchanted with his fiancée.

If Jacina thought she was unhappy that day, it was as nothing to the way she began to feel over the next few days.

The Earl never alluded to her outburst in the library. He simply no longer requested that she come and read to him alone. When their paths crossed in the castle and she curtsied with a soft 'my Lord,' he merely bowed his head coldly and moved on.

She was stricken, but after a while she tried to convince herself that it was for the best. Once he was married, the friendship would end anyway. She would return to her life in the village and all would be as it was before.

She tried to keep herself busy. She helped Nancy sort out the linen cupboards. She translated French recipes into English for cook. She visited poor and sick families on the estate and brought them provisions.

One afternoon, on her way to the cottage of a poor widow, she encountered Felice coming back along the path that led deep into the woods.

She was surprised. She knew that Felice disliked walking in the countryside. How then did she happen to be so far from the castle and on foot? She said nothing, however. She merely nodded 'hello' and waited for Felice to let her pass.

Felice was wearing a blue cape. Her hair was

dishevelled and her complexion heightened. She looked flustered to see Jacina. A nervous glance over her shoulder alerted Jacina to the possibility of a second party but when Jacina looked there was no-one.

"I have been walking in ze woods," said Felice in an unnaturally loud voice. "Ze air is very fresh."

"Yes, it is," said Jacina quietly. She tried to move on but Felice let out a loud cry.

"Oh, la, la, my shoes!" she lamented noisily. "Look, look, they are ruined."

Jacina looked down at the shoes. They did not seem at all ruined. She had the strangest feeling that Felice was deliberately trying to hold her there, but for what purpose she could not guess.

"What have you in ze basket?" asked Felice next.

"Some game pie," said Jacina. "For a family on the estate. The mother is ill."

Felice stared, then gave a short laugh. "My, you are so good, just like – " Her voice trailed off.

"Just like who?" asked Jacina.

Felice shrugged nonchalantly. "Pffoufft! It does not matter. Personne."

Jacina wondered who she meant by 'nobody.' Perhaps it was Crispian, her first fiancé, who Felice used to think so 'good'.

Felice was now looking keenly back along the path as if to satisfy herself of something.

"Excuse me," said Jacina. "I must get on."

Felice turned to her quickly. "What? Oh, yes. You may go now." She leaned in close to Jacina. "But – you will not tell zat you saw me in the wood, hein? The Earl might think it was – curious."

54

Jacina regarded her coolly. "It is not my business...to tell anyone what you do," she said.

"Then we are friends!" said Felice. She smiled sweetly and stood aside.

As Jacina continued along the path with her basket, she wondered where Felice had been to look in such disarray. Around a bend in the path lay a woodsman's deserted cottage. With a frown Jacina saw that the door was swinging open. She stepped up to the cottage and closed the door. It was no good letting the animals and chickens wander in.

Over the following days Jacina tried resolutely not to think of Felice or the Earl, but it was so hard when she was continually seeing them together. The evenings were the most difficult, when she went in to dine, but at least she was not alone with the engaged couple. There were always other guests, invited so that Felice could become acquainted with the local gentry .

The guests were always excitable and garrulous. Jacina knew that the Earl only invited them for the sake of Felice and in deference to the wishes of his grandfather, who had planned such gatherings leading up to the wedding. She knew it was torture for the Earl to put his blindness on public display.

Nobody noticed Jacina.

Every evening she ate in silence and excused herself at the earliest opportunity.

Then one evening, just before dessert, Monsieur Fronard tapped his glass and the Earl rose to his feet. The guests regarded him expectantly, while Jacina lowered her head as if at an impending blow. The Earl's strong voice carried all too clearly down the table. This was the announcement she had been dreading for days.

The date of the wedding was finally set!

*

Every day loaded carts drew up at the trade entrance of the castle. There were sacks of flour from the mill on the estate. There were bags of sugar and crates of eggs. There were boxes of late fruit and jars of sweetmeats. Cook was in her element. Her arms were always covered to the elbow in flour. She was determined to make it the most glorious wedding breakfast in the history of the castle.

The haberdasher came with bolts of silk and muslin and satin. The shoemaker came with swatches of leather. The glove-maker came and the milliner.

The dressmaker came.

Jacina watched the hustle and bustle from her window. She fervently hoped that the Earl might now find happiness.

Sometimes she sought refuge with Sarah. When Sarah brought out the caddy to make the tea, Jacina looked sadly at its painted scenes of India.

The Earl had once again become as distant to her as a dream.

One afternoon Sarah's arthritis was playing up. She asked Jacina to make the tea. As Jacina reached the caddy down, a thin packet of letters that had been lodged behind it fell to the floor.

Sarah noticed. "Those are letters Miss Felice wrote to me when Master Crispian was alive," she commented.

As Jacina picked up the letters, she could not help but notice the dainty handwriting.

Sarah said no more about Felice. She hardly ever mentioned Felice now and she never chatted about the forthcoming wedding.

As the day drew near, Jacina wished more and more that she could take herself back to her home in the village but she knew that was not possible. The house was locked up. The housemaid had gone with Doctor Carlton to Edinburgh. Besides, Jacina always obeyed her father's wishes. No matter what, she must remain at the castle.

She read and re-read letters from her father. He had written to say that though the Earl had invited him, he did not know whether he would be able to attend the wedding.

The afternoon before the wedding day Jacina was surprised by a knock at her bedroom door. It was Nancy. "Miss Felice wants to see you, Miss," she said. "In her room."

Jacina was too intrigued to refuse.

Felice had been given the room hung with yellow silk. When Jacina arrived dresses were strewn all over the carved oak bed. Hats and gloves lay about on chairs. Felice stood in front of a pier glass. The dressmaker fussed around her, arranging swathes of white satin in place. She was putting the final touches to her wedding dress.

"I wanted your opinion," said Felice. "What do you think of this dress?"

"It is...perfect," murmured Jacina, puzzled.

"Oh, I suppose it is alright, but really, ze workmanship is not as good as I could get in Paris or even London."

The dressmaker, mouth full of pins, flushed and tried to look as if she wasn't there.

Felice held something up for Jacina to see. "And what about these? Do these diamonds look good with zis white satin?"

Jacina glanced at the necklace that had briefly lain around her own neck and then looked away.

"Ideal," she said.

Felice regarded her curiously, her head on one side.

"You would like zis necklace to be yours, no?" she asked softly.

Jacina met her gaze in the glass.

"I am well aware that it can never be mine," she said simply.

Felice threw back her head and laughed gaily. "Oh how I am enjoying zis!" she exclaimed.

Jacina was confused. "En..enjoying...what?" she asked.

"Everything!" cried Felice. "Everything is better now!" She wiped her eyes as if she had been crying with amusement and waved a hand at Jacina. "Why don't you go away now, back to your dull old books!"

Jacina was bewildered. Felice Delisle was playing with her as a cat plays with a mouse and she could not understand why. Turning on her heels to leave, she found her way barred by the figure of Monsieur Fronard. He regarded her with a scowl. "What are you doing here?" he asked.

"I sent for her," said Felice airily.

"You sent for her?" repeated Fronard, raising his eyes to Felice where she stood by the pier glass.

"*Mais oui.* I get bored, you know, bored."

Fronard growled something that Jacina heard as "*Prenez guarde.*"

"*Take care!*"

Jacina had had enough. She pushed past Fronard and hurried back to her room, her spirits deeply disturbed.

What kind of creature was Felice Delisle? To have sent for Jacina and taunted her purely out of boredom! She had not seemed to consider it at all unseemly that Fronard should enter when she was being fitted for her wedding dress. What if the Earl found out?

With a chill Jacina found herself thinking the unthinkable.

Perhaps it suited Felice Delisle that the Earl of Ruven was blind!

*

That night Jacina could not sleep.

She tossed and turned in her bed. Whenever she closed her eyes she saw Felice Delisle holding up the diamond necklace. She heard that high-pitched laugh ringing through her.

Her heart was full of anguish. Was the Earl about to doom himself to an unhappy marriage? It might be so and yet there was nothing she could do to help him. He was in love with Felice Delisle, that was certain. No man could have been more solicitous of her happiness.

Jacina sat up. The room seemed so close and stuffy. She needed air, fresh air! Throwing aside the counterpane, she got out of bed and went to the window. She drew back the curtain. Moonlight poured into the room like a flood of silver. She opened the window catch and leaned out.

It had rained all day but now it had stopped. The air was cool and sweet. The moonlight touched the earth with filigree. The unutterably peaceful night seemed to beckon to the heart-sore Jacina. She dressed quickly, took up her cloak and left her room. She tiptoed through the corridors, not wishing to rouse anyone.

She had to take great care tugging at the front door. Once it was open, she hesitated and then found a stone to wedge the door, so it would not completely close behind her. She wanted to be able to get back in without having to summon one of the servants.

The woods on the other side of the moat seemed too dark to enter, despite the moonlight. She turned to the right

59

and followed along under the castle walls. A thin ribbon of light across the grass made her look up. The lamp in the Earl's chamber was still burning.

Sarah had remarked that recently the Earl seemed to sit up half the night.

Jacina pressed on and skirted the east tower. The moat was not so wide on this side of the castle. A wooden bridge led over it to a rose garden, a herb garden and an apple orchard. It also led to a pretty copse. A flagged path ran through the trees to a clearing wherein stood a stone folly. The folly was in the shape of a small, round temple, open to the elements on all sides.

Jacina often came here alone to read when the weather was warm enough. It had become her secret place.

The path that led to the clearing twisted through the copse, sometimes almost doubling back upon itself. She stepped lightly along, her cloak pulled close.

She was right to have come out! The sharp night air seemed to clear her troubled mind. The tranquillity of the landscape soothed her heavy heart.

All was well until she drew near the clearing. Then, to her astonishment, she heard the sound of voices ahead. She was not alone! She hesitated and then crept closer. The dome of the folly came into view. A few steps closer and she could see the clearing itself through the trees. It was bright under the moonlight and the two figures standing together in the folly were clearly outlined.

Monsieur Fronard and Felice Delisle!

Fronard had Felice's hands grasped in his. He spoke low and urgently. Felice shook her head and Fronard dropped her hands. He said something else and at this Felice threw back her head and gave a silvery laugh. Fronard put a finger under her chin and lifted her face to his. He leaned forward and kissed Felice Delisle full on the lips.

With a gasp Jacina drew herself deeper into the shadows. As she did so the edge of her cloak caught on a bush. The whole bush shook as she tugged her cloak free.

Fronard and Felice drew apart and looked her way.

Her heart in her mouth, she turned on her heels and stumbled back through the copse.

She did not know where she was going or what she would do when she got there. What *could* she do! All she could think of was Felice and Fronard embracing in the folly.

In her haste she took a wrong turning and slithered into a ditch. Icy water oozed up over the top of her ankle boots. Breathing heavily, she scrambled from the ditch and turned back onto the main path. Her feet were now soaking wet. Low branches lashed at her face as she ran. She broke from the copse just as the moon went sailing into a sudden mass of dark cloud.

The castle at least was still outlined against the sky and she raced toward it.

Reaching the moat she was thrown into confusion. Which way was the wooden bridge? It was too dark to see. Should she turn to the left or right?

Her head jerked up. Was that the snapping of a twig in the copse behind her? Her heart went chill in her breast. Suppose Fronard was coming after her? What would such a man do to prevent her reporting what she had seen? She had to take a chance. She must reach the safety of the castle.

Heart pounding she plunged to the left. It was the right decision. She found the wooden bridge and stumbled across. Reaching the castle in minutes she pushed at the heavy door. The stone she had left there tumbled aside.

Now she was running up the stairway, running without pause.

Who could she go to, who?

Even as she reached the top of the stairs, she knew. Sarah! Surely Sarah would listen to her.

She had barely breath left in her body by the time she reached the nursery. She fell against the door and beat upon it with her fists.

"Who's there?" called Sarah.

"It's me, it's me!"

"Jacina?"

The door was opened and Jacina stumbled with a cry into the old nanny's arms.

CHAPTER FIVE

Firelight flickered on the nursery wall. Jacina sat hunched in a chair, a blanket round her shoulders. Her boots and stockings lay drying on the hearth. She was clutching a mug of hot milk, from which she now and then took a small sip. Her voice was tremulous as she told her tale.

Sarah listened in grim silence.

When Jacina had finished the old woman turned her head and stared into the coals. Her face was sombre in the glow.

"I knew it from the first," she said at last.

"You...you did?" stammered Jacina.

Sarah looked at her. "Oh, I didn't know exactly what was going on. Mercy, no. But when the Earl brought Miss Felice up here to meet me, I thought at once she had the look of a minx on her." Sarah mused for a moment before continuing. "They say suffering makes the heart soften, but it seems to have had the opposite effect on Miss Felice Delisle. Or maybe it's that Fronard, leading her astray."

Jacina was staring at Sarah. She had just remembered

that encounter with Felice on the woodland path, when Felice had looked so dishevelled and had tried to keep her talking. She recalled the woodsman's cottage and how the door was swinging open as if someone had left in a hurry.

Was the cottage another of Felice and Fronard's trysting places?

She put down her mug slowly. "What must I do, Sarah?"

Sara's reply was unequivocal. "You must tell the Earl what you saw, my lovely. You must indeed tell him what you saw."

Jacina knew that Sarah was right but her heart sank. How was she to approach the Earl? She knew what Sarah did not, that it had been a while since she and the Earl had been alone together or enjoyed any kind of companionship. She had long been banished from his good graces. Even now her cheeks burned at the memory of that scene in the library when she had inadvertently offended Felice by wondering aloud at her relish for tragic love stories.

Or had it been so inadvertent? Might she not even then have secretly suspected that Felice was not all she seemed?

Jacina's thoughts were in a whirl. Whatever Felice was, the Earl was in love with her. How could Jacina possibly confront him with the lurid truth?

With a sudden small cry she buried her face in her hands.

Sarah watched anxiously. "Do you want that I should go tell the Earl, Jacina?"

Jacina straightened. "No, Sarah. You...you didn't witness it. I did. It is I who...who must go."

There was another reason for Jacina deciding that it must be she and she alone who went to the Earl. The Earl could well resent the messenger. Better then that the messenger be someone already out of his favour!

Having found her resolve she knew she must act without delay. Shrugging off her blanket, she leaned down to collect her boots and stockings from the hearth.

"But they're still damp!" exclaimed Sarah, when she saw what Jacina was doing.

"I know Sarah but it's getting late and...I have to go tonight. You know that."

Sarah sighed and sank back in her chair. Of course Jacina had to go tonight. Tomorrow would be too late.

Tomorrow the Earl and Felice Delisle would be wed.

*

The castle was very quiet as Jacina made her way to the Earl's study.

She knew that was where she would find him. She had seen the light shining from the study window. Sarah had said he sat up late.

When she came to the study she tapped very lightly upon the door. She did not want anyone other than the Earl to hear. There was no response. She was about to knock again when she heard footsteps coming up the stairs. She cast about her in dismay. Where could she hide?

There was nothing for it but to crouch down at the side of a large coffer that stood to the right of her in the passageway. She had to hope that whoever was approaching went to the left at the top of the stairs and not to the right. If they turned to the right and passed the coffer they could not fail to see her.

She saw the light of a lamp bob into view and squeezed further back against the wall.

The person carrying the lamp stopped outside the Earl's study and knocked loudly. Jacina's heart gave a thump as she heard the Earl's deep voice call out.

"Who's there?"

It thumped even harder when she heard the reply.

"Fronard."

Fronard! What was he doing here at this hour?

"Enter," said the Earl.

She heard the door open. The bobbing light vanished as Fronard went in to the study and closed the door behind him.

This was an unexpected turn of events. What should she do? The safest action would be to creep away now, while she had the opportunity. If Fronard came out and turned to his left down the passageway – as well he might, since his own room lay in that direction – he would pass the coffer. If Jacina was still there he would undoubtedly discover her.

She was frightened of Fronard. If the truth were told, she had been frightened of him from the first. His sharp eyes seemed to notice everything. There was a hint of cruelty in their gaze. She wondered if Felice was indeed the marionette, as Sarah had suggested, and Fronard the master.

Jacina knew she must not let her fear drive her away. If she did not tell the Earl what she had seen, then she would be consigning him to a marriage he might bitterly regret.

She stayed there in the passageway, praying that she would not be found out. The clock struck a quarter to the hour. She shrank further into the corner, shivering. The clock struck one. A few seconds later the study door opened.

"Goodnight, your Lordship," came the voice of Fronard.

He pulled the study door to, but she did not hear it close. Perhaps that was because her ears were full of the sound of her anxious heart. It beat so loudly in her rib cage, she was surprised Fronard himself did not hear it. A second later she thought with horror that he had, for the light from the lamp he carried remained motionless a few feet beyond her. He was standing still outside the Earl's door. Standing still and listening!

Jacina tried to stop her very breath.

At last the light began to bob again. It moved away from her and down the stairs.

Jacina let out a long sigh of relief and then rose awkwardly to her feet. Feeling stiff and cold, she stepped up to the study door.

It stood ajar. She gently pushed it wide. Her heart caught in her throat as she saw the Earl there before her. He was leaning with one arm on the mantelpiece, his face turned towards the fireplace. He could not see the flame of the fire, but he undoubtedly felt its warmth on his flesh.

He was in a long, black, velvet dressing gown. It was open to his breastbone and she saw the dark hair of his chest.

The sight of him made her feel faint. Trembling, she stepped forward. "My...my Lord."

His head snapped up. "Jacina?"

"Yes, my Lord. I...I have something important to tell you."

The Earl's reply was icy. "It does not surprise me, madam, that you do."

His words confused Jacina and his manner was so cold, she wanted to turn and flee. Yet Sarah had said this was the right thing to do and she must do it. She opened her mouth but could not speak. Instead a sob rose in her throat.

The Earl cocked his head as if he heard this. "Well?" he said impatiently.

The words came from her in a rush. "My Lord I...I

could not sleep. I needed air...I went out to the garden...to the folly, where I often go. I...I saw two people there. Monsieur Fronard and your fiancée Felice. I saw them together in a way that was not...they embraced, my Lord...they kissed...I wish I had not seen it, but...I did and...it cannot be right for them to...I felt you had to know...surely...you had to know.'

Her voice trailed off. Tears ran down her cheeks and she wiped them away with her sleeve.

"For...forgive me, my Lord."

"Forgive you?" The Earl's voice cut through the air like a blade. "Forgive you, this vicious tittle tattle? This odious slander? This clumsy attempt to blacken the name of the woman I am to marry?"

"My...my Lord?"

The Earl's face was a study in rage. The brows were thunderous. His unseeing eyes blazed with fury. His words burned into her like acid.

"Madam, Fronard himself has only just left me. He was at his window and saw you wandering in the garden. He has been much disturbed of late by your behaviour. He expected something of this sort from you. He told me how you have been   watching my fiancée – attempting to undermine her at every turn."

"But my L..."

"DO NOT INTERRUPT ME!"

He might as well have raised his hand to her. She began to shake before him. The room seemed to dance and turn about her.

The Earl sensed where she stood and advanced toward her, his harsh words falling like blows. "From the first you have displayed a jealousy of her position. Fronard told me how Felice even found you trying to steal the diamond necklace I had given her."

"No, no, my Lord," cried Jacina. " No. That is not..."

With a cry of anger, the Earl caught at her with one outstretched hand. His fingers settled around her throat. Even now, even though it was in seething fury, his touch made her swoon. She knew at that moment, she would willingly have died by his hand than so utterly lose his affection.

"Do you deny it?" he hissed.

His face so close to hers was a strange torture. She closed her eyes.

"I...deny it...my Lord."

His hot breath was upon her cheek. Even as she felt herself yielding in his grasp, the nature of his breathing changed. She opened her eyes.

There was sudden bewilderment in his unseeing gaze. His fingers on her throat slackened. For one moment – one moment in which her heart almost ceased to beat – his lips came close to hers. Then he loosened his grip and stepped back. He passed a hand across his brow.

"Be gone, be gone!" he muttered. He turned from her and walked unsteadily back to the fire.

"My Lord," she murmured, "please, my Lord..."

He rounded on her with a wild and violent cry. "Be gone, I say!"

Shaken to her very core, Jacina turned and fled.

*

Like an animal mortally wounded, she blundered along the corridors. Her breath scarcely sustained her, yet on she went. Finding almost by instinct the stairway that led to her room, she hung panting for a moment on the banisters, her breast heaving with sobs she dare not utter. Only the sound of a door opening below her gave her the strength to mount.

The door of her room was ajar. She flung herself across the room and onto her bed. At last she could freely give vent to her feelings. Loud sobs racked her body. She twisted and turned, her fingers clutching now at the counterpane, now at the pillow.

She could imagine no greater torment.

The man she so admired – nay, so adored – believed she was no more than a jealous and conniving rival to his fiancée!

Jacina lay there wrestling with her conscience. Had she for one moment felt relish in going to the Earl with her story? No, she had not! Had she hoped the Earl would cancel the wedding when he heard the truth about Felice? Yes, but she had hoped that for his sake, not her own. Had she for a second believed she would benefit from the Earl being disillusioned with his fiancée? No! No-one in their right mind could imagine that the heartbroken Earl would turn for comfort to the very woman who had been instrumental in destroying his happiness.

All she had wished to do was save the Earl from the clutches of Monsieur Fronard and the woman Jacina now believed was his creature, Felice Delisle.

That in the process she might inflict a wound on Felice had been, she had to admit this to herself, a source of some satisfaction.

Not because the Earl loved Felice but because Felice *did not love him*.

Jacina moaned as she realised that, whatever her intentions, she had ended up doing more harm than good. Unwittingly, she had helped drive the Earl further into the power of Fronard and Felice.

The Earl believed Fronard had acted to protect Felice from Jacina's wicked machinations. He believed Fronard to be honest and Felice innocent. What he believed Jacina to be, broke her heart.

Her own loud cries of despair frightened her. She turned and buried her face in the pillow. The pillow was soon drenched with tears.

As if in a sad mirror to her mood, heavy rain began to fall on the castle, the garden, the wood, the copse. Jacina barely heard it. She barely heard the wind rising, carrying more rain-swollen clouds over the neighbouring crags.

The wind tugged at the catch that she had not quite fastened when she closed the window earlier that night. The catch loosened and the window swung wide.

Chill air began to seep into the room.

Jacina did not notice. She lay in a daze, the world a shadow to her. She did not notice how numb her feet became in the damp boots. She did not notice how her fingers turned to ice.

She did not notice how, as the night wore on, fever took its burning grip upon her brow.

*

Steeple bells echoed through the frosty air. It was morning. Raindrops glistened on the boughs of trees. Pale yellow sunlight filled the sky and filtered through the stained glass windows of the Ruven family chapel, where guests had gathered for the wedding.

The wedding of the Earl of Ruven and Felice Delisle.

The Earl stood waiting at the altar. Tall and straight, he never once turned to look at the congregation. He seemed lost in his own thoughts.

Sarah sat at the back of the chapel, turning her head every time someone entered from the porch. She was looking for Jacina. Jacina had left the nursery last night determined to go to the Earl with her story. She had not returned to tell Sarah what happened. Sarah did not for one moment doubt that Jacina had indeed gone to the Earl. Why then was the wedding still taking place?

Perhaps the Earl was going to make an announcement at the altar? Sarah dismissed that idea as soon as it entered her head. The Earl was a gentleman. He would never humiliate Felice publicly.

The truth must be that he was so smitten with his fiancée he was prepared to marry her no matter what.

Sarah sighed. Then she turned her head at the sound of whispering by the church door.

Felice Deslisle was entering on the arm of Monsieur Fronard.

A gasp swept round the congregation at the sight of Felice. Even Sarah had to admit she looked beautiful. She was wearing a white satin dress with a long train. Her veil was held in place with a sparkling tiara and the Ruven diamonds gleamed about her long neck.

At the altar the Earl stiffened. He could hear the rustling of the train over the old stones of the aisle. He could also hear the steady tread of Fronard.

Fronard delivered the bride to the altar. Then he stepped into a front pew.

Sarah watched the ceremony quietly. Her lips pursed when the Earl slipped the ring on his bride's finger.

Felice lifted her veil to receive a kiss. Then the couple turned and started back down the aisle. Sarah noticed that as Felice passed Fronard she threw him a quick glance. Her eyes glittered like the diamonds at her throat. Beside her the Earl's face was set and unsmiling.

The chapel bells began to ring, loud and clear in jubilation.

In her room at Castle Ruven, Jacina opened her eyes.

Why were church bells ringing? Was there a wedding? She seemed to remember someone had said there was going to be a wedding. She tried to raise her head, but there was no strength in her at all. Her head fell back on the pillow. Her breath came in gasps.

Where was her father? He should be told that she did not feel well. Her head was so hot, so very hot. Yet her limbs felt leaden with cold.

Where was she? She was not at home. No, she was...in a castle. She remembered now. In a castle. Who else was here? Servants. Yes, there were servants. And someone called Sarah. There were other people too...she did not want to remember...she would not remember.

She fell into a doze. Then she was awake again. She had heard the sound of wheels and horses neighing. Perhaps it was Papa. Oh, she would be so happy to see Papa. Then came the sound of cheers. No, it could not be Papa, they would not be cheering for Papa. So who was it? Who was it being welcomed so noisily below?

An unbidden image floated before her of a tall, dark man with a bride on his arm. Jacina's head thrashed to and fro on the pillow as if to chase the image from her. She did not want to think about it. Her head was too hot to think. Thoughts hurt her brain. Better to sleep. Just sleep.

Jacina did not know how long she slept. When she woke again, she woke because a hand was on her brow and a face was bending over her. "Mercy me, mercy me," someone was saying.

The room was bright. It had the feeling of early afternoon.

Jacina felt a cool flannel pressed to her forehead. Slowly the figure above her swam into focus and she recognised Sarah.

"Sarah...I tried...the Earl...did not believe me...not believe me..."

"Hush now, my lovely. Hush now. You are not at all well."

Jacina felt Sarah lift her head and urge a beaker to her lips. Jacina took a few sips of a bitter liquid and then sank back upon the pillows.

Sarah had Nancy light a fire in the hearth. Then she got Jacina out of her dress – muddied at the hem from her nocturnal slide into the ditch – and into a clean night-gown. Jacina was barely aware of all this.

Sarah lay Jacina down and tucked the counterpane around her. She then drew a chair up beside the bed and settled down to keep watch.

Sometimes Jacina slept. Sometimes she started up with a cry or spoke incoherent thoughts.

Afternoon faded into dusk. Still Sarah sat on. A frown creased her forehead, as she listened to Jacina's ramblings. Finally she seemed to come to some decision. When Jacina drifted into an uneasy sleep, Sarah tiptoed quietly from the room.

A misty moon rose at the window.

Jacina's eyes opened. She saw the moon and wondered if it was a lamp placed on the sill. There was another lamp shining by the bedside. All seemed a shadow, nothing was real. She turned her head on the pillow as the door was pushed gently open to the sound of someone speaking.

"Where have you brought me, Sarah? Are we in the nursery? No, we can't be, we did not climb that high."

It was the Earl's voice.

Jacina heard it dimly. She recognised it as a voice that had caused her pain. She closed her eyes. She wanted to drift away again into a quiet, dark repose.

Sarah answered the Earl. "That's right, we are not in the nursery, Master Hugo. Be patient and you shall know all."

The Earl's tone was bemused. " I came as you bid, but you must remember the ball begins in less than an hour. I have much to do. What game are you playing with your old charge?"

"It is no game," said Sarah grimly. "Come forward, sir. Give me your hand." Gently but firmly, Sarah guided the hand of the Earl and laid it on Jacina's hot brow.

The Earl gave a start. "What's this?"

"Your handiwork, Master Hugo."

"What do you mean? Who lies here?"

"Jacina," said Sarah quietly.

"Jacina!" cried the Earl, pulling away his hand.

His voice was so close now, so loud, that it shattered Jacina's numbed sensibilities. She knew in an instant who was there beside her. "My...Lord..." she mumured.

The Earl gave a groan and staggered back.

"She is sick, Master Hugo," said Sarah. "Sick with despair. She came to me last night with what she had seen. She didn't know what to do, poor creature. T'was I who told her to go to you. I, who've had my own suspicions about Felice Delisle. Why should I your old nanny, wish you harm? I believed and continue to believe Jacina. She has the truest heart of any I know. And you – a clumsy brute, though it do hurt me to say it and though the saying of it should lose me the roof over my head – you have broke that heart cruelly."

The Earl gave another groan and covered his face with his hand.

Jacina tried to raise herself in the bed. "My...Lord...I

did not want...to hurt you. I did not..."

The Earl felt for her hand. "Be calm, now, Jacina. Be calm. I was angry with you but I am angry no longer. I believe you." He turned to Sarah. "Have you given her anything for this fever?"

"I have. I will give her more now. It is a potion that works wonders."

The Earl nodded. "Good. We will speak more but now I must go. The guests are arriving."

He quickly kissed Jacina's hand before laying it gently down. He then found his way to the door and opened it. His valet stood waiting outside to guide him down.

"Master Hugo," Sarah called after him.

The Earl half turned. "Yes, Sarah?"

"What will you do, sir, about this business?"

The Earl's voice was like steel as he replied. "Rest assured, Sarah, I will deal with the matter. I will deal with the matter this very night."

With that, the door closed behind him.

CHAPTER SIX

Jacina lay listening as musicians tuned their instruments in the ballroom below.

The wedding party in the morning was small, as the Earl had wished, but the ball that evening would be well attended. All the most prominent families of the district were invited.

Coaches were already rolling up to the castle entrance. There were squeals as ladies gathered up their skirts and hurried to get in out of the rain that had begun to fall.

Jacina turned her head on her pillow and sighed.

Her fever had abated since the visit of the Earl. This was partly due to the bitter black potion Sarah had administered and partly due to her enormous relief of spirits, once she knew that the Earl believed her.

She had even begun to feel hungry and Sarah had immediately gone to the kitchen to order her some soup.

The orchestra below struck up a waltz. As Jacina watched the firelight shadows on the wall, they appeared to dance in time to the music. She wished she was recovered enough to go to the ball. Then her brow knit with concern.

The music was playing and the guests were arriving, but that did not mean all was well!

She had dimly registered the Earl's parting words. *I will deal with the matter this very night.* Now these words began to haunt her.

In what way would the Earl deal with the matter? What could he possibly do tonight when the castle was so full of guests?

If Felice was in love with Fronard – as she surely was – then why had she still resolved to marry the Earl. The injuries he sustained in India had provided her with the perfect excuse to withdraw from the marriage had she so wished.

If Fronard was in love with Felice – as he surely was – then why was he happy to see her married off to someone other than himself?

Could it be that they simply planned to continue their liaison after the marriage, whilst at the same time enjoying all the comforts that the wealth of the Earl would provide?

At this moment the door opened and Nancy entered, her face bright red from having run all the way up from the kitchen with her message.

"I'm to tell you, Miss, that Sarah's decided to make up a broth from fresh. So she'll be a half hour more."

"Thank you, Nancy. Are you busy below?"

"Oh, Miss, it's bedlam. It's all got to be ready for supper at nine. What a feast they'll have though! There's wild boar – it's been roasting on a spit all day – and pheasant and jugged hare and oysters. I sneaked away one of them oysters to have a taste but I didn't like it, Miss. It were just a mouthful of seawater."

As she chattered Nancy began to sway to the strains of

the waltz floating up from the ballroom below.

"Ooh, Miss, aren't them tunes lovely? There's not been a ball here since I came. The old Earl didn't go in for them."

"Have you seen the ballroom, Nancy?" Jacina asked.

"I peeped in through the French windows from the garden, Miss. It's like a fairy-tale. There's hundreds of candles in them – candelabras – and there's a gold saucer round each candle to catch the drips. Which is a good thing. I heard at the Duchess of Marlcombe's ball the wax dripped onto the bare shoulders of the ladies below and scalded them something awful."

"Did you see the Earl and his...his wife there?"

"They were greeting guests, Miss, at the door. I'd have liked to stay longer but that *Monsewer* appeared. He lit a cigar and stood there smoking and watching through the windows too. I crept away. I didn't want him seeing me. He's a skulker, he is. I was polishing silver in the pantry this morning and there he was skulking inside the gun room!"

Jacina sat up with a jolt.

"The gun room?"

"Yes, Miss."

"Did he...did he take a pistol or anything?"

"I didn't see one on him, Miss, but what else was he in there for? I don't trust him one bit, I'd – Oh, Miss Jacina!" Nancy's hand flew to her mouth. "Miss Jacina, what are you doing?"

Jacina had pushed back the bedclothes and slid her legs to the floor. "Getting up," she said firmly.

"But what for?" cried Nancy.

"To go...to the ball," said Jacina. She hoped she sounded stronger than she felt

"You can't do that, Miss!" exclaimed Nancy.

"I can and...I will," said Jacina. "But you must...help me. Before Sarah comes. Would you bring me...my dress...from the wardrobe? Please!"

Nancy hesitated. Then she went to the wardrobe and opened it. "Which one, Miss?"

Jacina was struggling out of her nightgown. "My...best. The blue muslin."

Nancy brought the dress over to Jacina.

"Help me put it on," urged Jacina.

She held up her arms. Nancy slipped the muslin dress over her head and then started fastening the hooks.

"Hurry, Nancy. Hurry."

"It's these hooks, Miss. My fingers is all thumbs!"

At last it was done. Jacina moved unsteadily to the pier glass to take a look. She was shocked at what she saw. Her hair was tangled. Her cheeks and lips were pale as chalk. Her eyes held no lustre.

She took up her hairbrush for an instant and then put it down. It could not be helped. She had no time to prettify herself. Sarah might return at any moment and Jacina knew she did not have the strength to defy the old nanny in person.

Nancy was folding up Jacina's nightdress.

"Nancy?"

"Yes, Miss?"

"Is there any sign of Sarah coming up?"

Nancy went over to the door and looked out. "No, Miss."

"Thank you Nancy," said Jacina.

"Miss Jacina?"

"Yes, Nancy?"

"You won't tell no-one about me sneaking the oyster, will you?"

Jacina gave a weak smile. "No, Nancy, of course I won't."

With that she stepped out into the corridor and descended the tower steps.

At first her legs felt as if they would give way beneath her at any moment. Every five steps or so she had to stop and lean on a table or against the wall. As she progressed however, she grew stronger.

She began to move with greater confidence.

At the top of the main stairway she stopped and peeped over the banisters into the great hall below.

The servants had risen before dawn to decorate the hall under the stern eye of Jarrold. The walls were bedecked with ribbons and sprays of flowers stood on the consoles. Candles flared in garlanded sconces.

The entrance door was flung wide open. Jarrold stood outside waiting to greet the coaches.

Jacina glanced at herself in the gilded mirror that hung at the head of the stairway. She still looked ghostly. On an impulse she plucked a white flower from a spray arranged on the table in front of the mirror. She fixed the flower in her hair and then slowly descended.

She could hear music and laughter as she approached the ballroom. Its doors were wide open and dancers whirled by in the bright light beyond. The brightness spilled down the centre of the corridor like a golden carpet.

Jacina stopped in her tracks. She moved into the shadows.

The Earl and Felice stood just inside the door. They were greeting a guest, Lord Bulling, whom Jacina recognised from one of the many suppers she had attended at the castle.

There was no sign of Fronard.

The Earl looked very distinguished in his dark frock coat. Felice looked stunning in a scarlet gown threaded with gold. Her amber eyes glittered at Lord Bulling over the top of her open fan.

It was obvious the Earl had not yet confronted her with what he knew.

The music ended with a flourish. There was scattered applause and then the ladies were led from the floor by their partners. All the dancers were hot and flushed from their exertions.

Jacina heard Lord Bulling ask the Earl if he might claim the next dance with his wife.

"By all means," said the Earl dryly.

Felice snapped her fan shut. She cast a dazzling smile at Lord Bulling and took his proffered arm. He led her proudly onto the floor just as the orchestra struck up and another waltz began.

The Earl stood at the door, half turned towards the corridor. He seemed lost in thought. Jacina watched him for a moment. Then she slipped quietly forward to the Earl's side. "My...my Lord."

He gave a start. "Jacina? What the deuce are you doing here? What are you thinking of, putting your health at risk like this?"

A worried frown creased his brow. Without thinking – as if their relations had returned to the ease of former days – Jacina put a reassuring hand on his arm. When the Earl felt her touch it seemed for a moment that a tremor passed through his body. Before she could wonder at it, the Earl had straightened.

"Come, Madam. What explanation have you for quitting your bed?"

"Forgive me but I...I had to, my Lord. I had to warn you."

"Warn me? Those are strong words."

"Yes, my Lord. But you see...Fronard...may have...a pistol. He was...in the gun room...this morning."

The Earl was suddenly still as a stone. "The gun room? Who saw him there?"

"Nancy, my Lord."

The Earl's brows drew together as he pondered. "But why should he feel it necessary to have a gun? As far as he knows, I remain ignorant of his – his attachment to my wife."

Jacina could not help but flinch at the sound of the word 'wife' on the Earl's lips. Whatever might ensue, that was who Felice was now. The Earl's wife and the Countess of Ruven. No power on earth could take those titles from her.

"Jacina," said the Earl suddenly. "How strong do you feel?"

"I feel...very well, my Lord."

"Mmmn. Well, I must believe you, for I need you to be my eyes. Jacina, will you pay me the compliment of waltzing with me?"

"I should be...delighted, my Lord."

She took the Earl's arm and he led her – by instinct alone – through the crowd and onto the floor. There, the Earl asked her in a low voice to draw near. Trembling, Jacina obeyed. When he felt her close, the Earl gently put an arm about her waist and drew her to his breast.

They glided out into the midst of the dancers.

Jacina melted in the Earl's firm embrace. They swept about the ballroom in perfect harmony. The Earl moved with confidence, his step never faltering. She felt his breath on her hair.

"What is this?" he asked.

"My Lord?"

The Earl put up his hand and drew from her hair the white flower she had placed there before entering the ballroom.

"Oh, the flower...I used it as...an ornament, my Lord."

"What colour is it?"

"White, my Lord."

"I can imagine it in your red-gold hair," the Earl smiled.

Jacina smiled in return, though he could not see her. How she wished they could dance forever! She was hardly aware of other faces, other figures, whirling by. Then the Earl spoke again, gently into her ear.

"Jacina, do you see my wife still dancing?"

Jacina let her eyes rove about the floor. They widened when she finally caught sight of Felice. "She is dancing, my Lord, but not...not with Lord Bulling. She has found...a new partner."

The Earl's voice was low and contained in response. "And who is it, pray?"

"Monsieur...Fronard."

"What the deuce!" cried the Earl. "Does she dishonour me in public now?"

Jacina winced.

"What is the matter?" asked the Earl quickly.

"You are...hurting...my hand, my Lord."

The Earl loosened his grip instantly. "Forgive me," he said.

They stood still in the centre of the floor.

"It is time," said the Earl menacingly. "Lead me to them."

Jacina hesitated. She gazed up at his darkening eyes and fear gripped her heart in a vice. What did the Earl propose to do? Sensing her hesitation, the Earl crushed her almost violently to him. "Do this for me," he breathed.

Reluctantly, Jacina took his arm and started to move with him through the dancers. At that moment the waltz ended. There was scattered applause.

Fronard and Felice were among those who waited on the floor for the next dance to begin. They talked in an intimate manner, heads close together. As Felice threw her head back in a laugh, she saw Jacina and the Earl approach.

"The Earl," she murmured quickly to Fronard.

Fronard turned abruptly. His lips curled in a barely disguised sneer at the sight of the Earl's hand on Jacina's arm.

"I thought you were eeel," said Felice to Jacina.

Jacina supposed that by 'eeel' Felice meant *ill*.

"I am better now," she said simply.

"Do not concern yourself with Miss Carlton's health, Madame," said the Earl to Felice. "Concern yourself rather with your own behaviour."

Felice gave a gay laugh. "My behaviour? Mais pourquoi?"

"Because, Madame, it is too brazen for my taste."

Felice and Fronard exchanged a quick look.

"What is this – brazen?" asked Felice.

The Earl spoke in a controlled, cold tone. "It means, Madame, that your conduct does not befit your station."

Felice tapped her fan against her lower lip. "I do not understand what you are saying," she shrugged.

"I am saying," said the Earl, "that your treachery is discovered. You were seen in the folly. With your – with Monsieur Fronard."

Felice paled. Fronard slowly levelled a black gaze upon Jacina and she shrank before him.

"Fronard," said the Earl.

"Monsieur?" said Fronard, his eyes still on Jacina.

The Earl stepped nearer to Fronard. It was as if he were measuring the distance between them.

"You will understand," he said, "that I must demand satisfaction?"

He removed a glove as he spoke. Jacina, looking from one man to the other, did not for a moment grasp his intent. Only when the Earl struck Fronard's cheek with his glove did she realise. She almost fainted with horror.

An immediate hush ran through the ballroom. The musicians, about to play, lowered their instruments and stared. The Earl, the blind Earl, had challenged Fronard to a duel! Surely this was the most foolhardy act imaginable!

Jacina cast wildly about her as if seeking a sane human being, someone who would talk the Earl out of this idiocy.

It should be his wife. But she seemed as shocked as Jacina. It should be Fronard, if he had any decency in him at all. But Fronard wore the air of a man who could not believe his luck.

"Nothing would give me greater pleasure," he leered, "than to accept."

"Tomorrow at dawn?" said the Earl coldly.

"Tomorrow at dawn," said Fronard. He bowed, cast an unreadable glance at Felice and walked away.

The crowds parted in wonder to let him through and then drew together again to gaze on the Earl, Felice and Jacina. Suddenly Felice began to laugh hysterically.

"Felice!" said the Earl sharply. "Stop it!"

Felice went on laughing.

"Control yourself, for God's sake, Madame," said the Earl.

Felice stopped laughing. She stepped forward in a seeming daze and buried her head against the Earl's chest. He stood as if stunned. Over her bowed head, his eyes looked almost haunted.

"Jacina, Jacina," he mumured at last. "Are you there? Can you – lead – us out?"

Without hesitation – numb and unable to speak – Jacina took his hand. With his free hand, the Earl grasped Felice.

The three of them made their way to the door.

Guests looked at each other. It was obvious the ball had ended.

Jarrold, having been summoned from the Great Hall, stood aside to let the Earl and the women pass. He then hurried over and spoke to the musicians, who began to pack up their instruments.

"Take us to the stairs, Jacina," said the Earl.

Felice seemed to be allowing herself to be mutely led. Then suddenly, at the top of the stairs, she wrenched herself free of the Earl's grasp and threw herself down before him.

"Husband – you must believe me – Monsieur Fronard, his – his attentions were – never welcome. Always I was resisting him. I was – afraid of him. I do not lie. My husband – only once were his lips on mine. I am – pure for you."

Jacina could not believe her ears. She scanned the Earl's face anxiously but could not read his expression. Was it possible he believed Felice?

The Earl hesitated. Then he lowered a hand and gently pulled Felice to her feet.

Jacina caught a sudden scent of heady perfume, sickly sweet as funeral lilies. Her vision swam as she watched Felice put a hand to the Earl's face.

"You are my husband," Felice whispered huskily. "Zis is our wedding night. Come, come to our bed now. Prove you believe me."

The Earl caught at her wrist. He held it tight, his jaw clenching and unclenching.

"That is a pleasure I must forgo for the present, Felice," he said at last. "How can I lie with you tonight when tomorrow you may be a widow?"

Hearing these last words, Jacina gave a great cry and fell to the floor.

She neither saw the figure of Sarah hurry forward from the shadows, nor felt the strong male arms that lifted her. Lifted and carried her gently and carefully to her own so recently abandoned bed.

All that was left behind at the top of the stairs was a white flower, crushed violently underfoot.

*

A cold mist hung over the grass. The moon still hovered in a hazy dawn sky. Outside the castle, a black horse and a grey stood waiting, their nostrils steaming in the cold air.

The Earl came quickly down the steps, pulling on his

gloves. He was followed by his valet. The valet held the black horse while the Earl mounted and then himself mounted the grey. With a nod from the Earl the two horses and their riders wheeled round and set off over the stone bridge.

A moment later a gig drove up to the castle entrance. It was driven by one of the stable boys. He sat whistling under his breath.

The castle door opened again and Jarrold ushered out two cloaked women. They hurried down the steps and into the gig. Jarrold muttered something to the boy, who stopped whistling and climbed down from the driver's seat. Jarrold then got up in his stead. He cracked the whip and the gig set off.

In the gig, Jacina stared resolutely ahead. She did not need to look back to know that Felice stood watching from a window of the Great Hall. She had expressed no desire to be present at the duel while Jacina could not for her life have stayed away. She had told Sarah fiercely that if no-one would order her a gig, then she would walk by herself to the appointed place.

In the end Sarah had prevailed upon Jarrold to let herself and Jacina ride with him.

Jarrold was bringing the pistol case.

Today, one man would fall, injured or killed. No-one at the castle believed it would be Fronard. How could it be, when his opponent was blind?

Nobody but Jacina and Sarah was clear as to the reason for the duel.

Jacina sat in the gig with her hands in her lap. She had only one thought in her head, one prayer on her lips. *Let me be his eyes somehow. Let me be his eyes.* She knew it was impossible yet all her will was trained to this one end.

To save the Earl by her very presence.

The gig rolled through the wood and turned off the path into a glade. The black horse and the grey stood tethered to a tree stump. Fronard and the Earl stood in the centre of the glade but apart. Fronard had his back to them. He was smoking a cigar.

Jacina shuddered when she saw the doctor sitting in his gig. He had been summoned from Ruvensford village. She wished it was her father and not his locum.

Jarrold helped Jacina and Sarah from the gig. After glancing around for a moment the two ladies withdrew under a giant oak to watch the proceedings.

Jarrold carried the pistol case over to the Earl's valet – serving as the Earl's second – and the steward, who had reluctantly agreed to second Fronard.

The Earl and Fronard removed their cloaks. Jarrold opened the pistol case for Fronard and the Earl to choose their weapons. The Earl ran his hand over the pistols. Fronard picked them up and examined them, a faint smile playing on his lips.

Then the duellists stood back to back. At a word from Jarrold they started on their paces. The Earl walked in as straight a line as Fronard, his head held high. He never hesitated, never stumbled.

Jacina could not tear her eyes from him.

The men turned and raised their pistols.

The Earl had the first shot. He raised his pistol straight before him, but Jacina was sure it was not levelled directly at Fronard. She twisted her hands together.

Please God let him not miss.

Fronard, standing with the oak in his view, caught sight of Jacina. He could not resist baiting her.

"Ah! You have come, Miss Jacina, to say good-bye to your friend!"

It was a foolish thing for him to do. The Earl cocked his head and slowly moved his pistol to the right, towards the sound of Fronard.

Jacina noticed the adjustment and hope flooded her heart.

The shot reverberated over the trees. Wood pigeons burst from amid the leaves, calling in alarm.

Fronard staggered but did not fall. He glanced at his shoulder as a red stain appeared there on his pale grey shirt. With an angry snarl he raised his pistol. Jacina felt the shot in her very being.

The Earl's head snapped back and he fell.

Jacina cried out and ran towards his prone body, but Jarrold and the doctor were there before her. She caught a glimpse of a bloodied forehead and then the doctor waved her back. She was caught sobbing in the arms of the Earl's valet who had joined the group around the Earl. Sarah hobbled up a moment later.

"Is he dead, is he dead?" Jacina moaned.

The doctor pressed his ear to the Earl's chest. Then he felt for his pulse. "He is still breathing," he said.

"Thank God," cried Jacina in relief. "THANK GOD!"

The doctor hurriedly bound the Earl's brow with a white cloth. "Let us get back to the castle" he then said. "He may be saved."

Nobody thought of Fronard.

The valet and Jarrold carried the Earl's body to the gig. Sarah followed, her arm supporting Jacina.

"The ladies can ride in my gig," said the doctor. He looked round and then gave an exasperated cry. "Where the devil – ?"

The doctor's gig had gone. With it had gone Fronard.

They now noticed the steward, rising with a groan from the grass.

"What happened?" asked Jarrold with a frown.

The steward explained. "Although it was evident the Earl was hit the first time, still that scoundrel Fronard raised his pistol to fire again. I heard him muttering – '*finish it, finish it*'. I wrestled with him and managed to snatch the pistol, but as I turned he hit me on the back of the head with something hard. I don't know what. I went down, but luckily fell on the pistol – so he hasn't got that."

Jarrold and the others thanked the steward warmly for his actions. It was clear that Fronard had intended to ensure that the Earl was dead with a second bullet.

Now they had to fly like the wind to the castle to save the Earl.

The steward elected to ride the Earl's black horse. The valet rode the grey. The doctor and the two ladies settled in the remaining gig with the Earl. Jarrold took the reins. The whip lashed through the air and the horses set off at a gallop.

The Earl's head lay in Jacina's lap. With trembling fingers, she brushed the hair back from his unconscious brow.

For this moment, he was hers.

For the whole drive back through the damp woods, as the sky grew lighter, he was hers.

Only at the castle was he torn from her.

Jacina had to force herself not to resist as Jarrold, the valet and the steward lifted the Earl from her arms. She climbed carefully down after him and then turned to help Sarah. Once alighted, Sarah hurried off to the kitchen entrance. She was going to order hot water and towels to be brought to the Earl's chamber.

The men began to climb the castle steps with their burden. The doctor hurried alongside, keeping an anxious eye on his patient.

Suddenly above them the castle door was flung open and Felice appeared. When her eyes fell on the unconscious Earl, they widened.

"He is not dead, Countess," said the doctor quickly. "There is hope."

With a great cry Felice collapsed weeping on her husband's body.

Jacina watched numbly from the foot of the steps.

"We must get him to his chamber, Countess," urged the doctor.

Felice allowed herself to be drawn from the Earl. She took a handkerchief from her sleeve and began dabbing the tears from her cheek. Her hand abruptly stayed as she caught sight of Jacina starting up the castle steps. She watched for a moment and then turned sharply on her heels.

As Jacina arrived at the top of the steps, the heavy oak door was slammed firmly in her face.

CHAPTER SEVEN

All day the Earl lay unconscious.

The bullet had entered his head over the left brow. The locum thought it had travelled under the skin and lodged at the back of the skull. He did not consider himself experienced enough to operate so a surgeon from Carlisle was sent for.

While awaiting his arrival everyone in the castle was subdued. There was little chatter in the kitchens. The servants went about their duties with long faces.

The corridor outside the Earl's chamber was as silent as the tomb.

As dusk fell a figure could be seen flitting through the castle like a ghost, candle in hand. It was Jacina.

She had waited all day and could wait no longer. She was desperate to see the Earl and judge for herself what chance he had of living. Sarah had told her that a nurse had been summoned from the village to sit with the Earl. Surely the nurse would not object if Jacina crept in to see him?

She reached the Earl's chamber and knocked softly.

She heard footsteps in the room beyond. The door opened and there before her stood – the Countess Felice! Jacina recoiled in dismay.

"What do you want?" asked Felice coldly.

"I c..came to see the Earl."

"You came to see my *husband*, hein?"

"Y..your husband, yes. I j..just wanted to..."

Felice cut her off icily. "You are not welcome here. My husband is lying eeel because of your meddling. If he dies it will be *your fault*. Do you understand, Mademoiselle? Your fault!"

Jacina stepped back from the doorway. She stood for a moment, her breast heaving. Then she turned and stumbled back to her room.

The candle guttered out in her hand.

All that night and next morning the Earl's chamber was guarded by the Countess. She dismissed the nurse from the village and allowed no-one other than the doctor to enter. She seemed determined to nurse her husband herself. Everyone agreed that she was proving herself an exemplary wife. Fronard had been a bad influence. With him gone Felice was herself again.

Jacina in her torment did not know what to think. Was it possible Felice really loved the Earl after all?

She remembered Felice weeping over the Earl's body when he was brought wounded to the castle.

Perhaps Felice had been telling the truth, when she said Fronard had been importunate with her, that his attentions had been unwelcome. It had not looked that way in the folly that night, but perhaps Jacina had misread the situation. Perhaps she had been wrong all along. This thought threw her into a fever of remorse.

'*If he dies it will be your fault*'. How could she blame Felice for those bitter words? They were only too true. If she had not gone on that moonlit walk...if she had not seen Fronard and Felice seemingly embrace...if she had not spoken of it to Sarah and the Earl...then the Earl would not now be hovering at death's door.

She sat for hours at her window, her eyes glued to the road. She was willing the Ruven coach to appear, bringing the surgeon from Carlisle.

Her watch was finally rewarded, when she saw the Ruven coach come racing towards the castle. It drew to a halt, the horses panting and steaming. The surgeon leapt out and ran up the steps with his gladstone bag.

Three hours later the good news flew through the castle. The bullet had been removed. The Earl had regained consciousness and was out of danger. There was no permanent damage.

Jacina felt faint with relief. She pressed her hands together and gave a prayer of thanks.

The surgeon left before supper. He declared himself satisfied with the Earl's condition. A week of rest and he would be able to resume normal life.

Jacina was at last able to relax. She fell into a deep sleep and was only wakened by Nancy bringing her some supper on a tray. Nancy was about to leave, when she suddenly thrust a hand into her apron pocket. "I nearly forgot, Miss. This is for you." She handed Jacina a note, bobbed a curtsey and left.

Dear Jacina, the note read, *the doctor ordered the Countess to take some rest so I am sitting with the Earl tonight. He has asked for you. Come after ten. Sarah.*

Jacina coloured as she stared at the note.

He has asked for you.

What did this mean? Was he going to reprimand her for all the trouble she had set in motion? If so, she did not care. Even to hear his voice, stern and cold, was better than not hearing it at all.

She waited in a fever of excitement until ten o'clock struck. This was the hour when the household usually retired. She lit a candle and, shielding it with one hand, opened the door. The corridor was empty. Indeed the whole castle seemed quiet as the grave. She saw no-one on her journey except a maid at the end of a corridor, carrying a jug of hot water towards the Countess's chamber.

The door to the Earl's chamber was ajar. Jacina gave a soft knock and pushed it open.

She had never been in this room before and for a moment its opulence took her breath away. Scarlet brocade curtains were drawn over the windows. The walls were hung with rich tapestries. Chairs were covered with blue damask.

The room was full of shadows. Candles flickered in silver candlesticks and a fire burned in the grate.

Sarah sat dozing in a wing chair.

Jacina hesitated and then tiptoed to the side of the large four poster bed.

The Earl lay in almost complete shadow under the canopy. His open eyes were like dark pools. A white bandage tinged with red bound his brow.

"Jacina?" he murmured as she gazed sorrowfully at him.

"My..my Lord," she started. "How did you...know?"

The Earl gave a smile. "You think I do not recognise the tread of my little helper?"

Jacina had not expected such a gentle tone. A tear spilled from her eye and trickled down her cheek. She wiped the tear away. "My...my Lord...I am sorry to have been the cause of so...so much discord. I thought I was...was acting for the best..."

The Earl raised his hand. "Hush, Jacina, hush. It is all forgotten. I believe Fronard to be the villain of the piece, not you. He had an unhealthy hold over my wife. You acted in all sincerity and that is why I asked you to come to me. I want to reassure you. Nobody knows of your role in this affair – except of course Sarah. Nobody blames you."

"Th..thank you, my Lord." Her voice was choked and she had to wait a moment before she could speak again. "Is there...any news of Fronard, my...my Lord?"

"None," said the Earl grimly. "The gig he took was found abandoned two miles further along the road, but he himself has disappeared into thin air."

Jacina digested this news. Wherever Fronard was, she hoped with all her heart he would never return to Castle Ruven.

"I am so glad that you are better, my Lord," she said.

"I am indeed better," said the Earl. "In fact, I shall soon be well enough to travel."

"T..travel, my Lord?"

"My wife has suggested that she and I spend some time in Switzerland. She is convinced the mountain air would aid my recovery. She will travel ahead to find a chateau for us to rent. I will follow on later."

"Oh," said Jacina faintly.

That Felice had won back the Earl's trust, she accepted. That the Countess planned to take the Earl away from England was, however, an unexpected blow.

Switzerland seemed like the far side of the moon to Jacina.

"Will you b..be away a long time?" she asked.

"Why, Jacina," the Earl teased, "it sounds as if you will miss me!"

Jacina blushed. "But I..I will, my Lord."

The Earl was silent for a moment. "Who knows what will transpire," he murmured at last. He turned his head away and Jacina realised it was in an attempt to hide a grimace of pain.

Without thinking, she put her hand consolingly over his where it lay on the counterpane.

The Earl started at her touch. Then, slowly, his fingers closed over hers. He turned back to her, his features relaxing. She tried to draw her hand away, but he held it fast. Her heart began to pound as he raised her hand to his lips.

Jacina felt she would faint with the sensation that swept through her body. If only her hand could remain in his forever! His grasp was so strong! She felt herself drawn closer and closer.

"Forgive this display of weakness before a trusted friend," murmured the Earl.

A trusted friend! That was all she was to the Earl, all she would ever be. Jacina closed her eyes. She reproached herself for imagining even for one second that she could be anything more.

As Sarah stirred in her chair, the Earl released Jacina's hand.

"You must leave now," he said.

"Y..yes, my Lord." As she opened the door she paused to glance back at the bed.

The Earl lay hidden from her in its shadowy depths.

*

Jacina was cheered a week later to receive a letter from her father.

Doctor Carlton wrote that he was coming to fetch her home. His friend the professor had recovered and the cholera epidemic was over. He was no longer required in Edinburgh. He would arrive on Sunday.

Jacina told Nancy she was finally going home and Nancy said sadly that everyone in the castle would miss her.

Jacina spent the afternoon sorting out her effects. When she went down to supper that evening, she found the castle in an uproar.

It seemed that the Countess had decided she would set out for Switzerland the very next day.

Maids were packing for the journey. Laundry maids were busy getting under-garments washed and dried. Footmen had been sent to retrieve trunks from the attic.

Jacina heard all about the preparations from Nancy.

"She's taking everything with her," said Nancy. "Cloaks. Gowns. Muffs and fox furs. Satin slippers. All her jewellery. Rubies and emeralds and pearls. Not to mention them Ruven diamonds. You'd think she weren't coming back for years."

Jacina wondered sadly if that was indeed Felice's plan.

The next morning the Great Hall was full of trunks and hatboxes. Footmen hoisted luggage onto the coach that was to carry the Countess to the railway station at Carlisle. She would reach Dover by midnight and sail for France at daybreak.

Jacina stood on the staircase watching the hustle and bustle below.

A maid hurried down the stairs with a travelling bag. The Countess followed, wearing a red fur lined cloak. She paused on the step above Jacina and stood there, drawing on her red gloves. "So you go tomorrow also," she murmured. "Tsk! How lonely my poor husband will be!" With that she swept on down the stairs. Jacina stared after her in surprise.

The Earl appeared on the arm of his valet. He had come to say goodbye to his wife. The bandage was still around his brow and low over his eyes. He looked pale.

The Countess was tall but even she had to stand on tiptoe to kiss her husband goodbye. She put her arms around his neck and pressed her lips to his.

Jacina found herself looking away.

"A bientôt!" said Felice. She gave a little wave and walked out to the waiting coach.

That night a gale arose. The mournful sound echoed down the chimneys. Trees tossed their heads wildly. Jacina thought of sailing across the channel in weather like this. It would not be pleasant.

All the next day she waited for her father, but he did not come. At six o'clock there was a loud banging at the main door. It was a messenger for Jacina. He had ridden all the way from Melrose. An elm had been uprooted in the gale and had fallen on the inn where her father was lodging for the night on his way home. As Jacina paled, the messenger hastened to add that her father was unharmed, but there were many injured and the doctor felt obliged to remain and help. He thought he would be detained a few days.

Once she was reassured that her father was safe, Jacina felt proud that he should elect to stay behind and help others.

That afternoon she decided to go and get a book from the library. She had packed all her own books in preparation for going home.

When she entered the library she found to her surprise that the curtains were drawn. Only the glow of the fire alleviated the gloom. She started to open one of the curtains when a voice from behind startled her.

"Leave them closed, please."

The Earl sat deep in the shadows in a high back chair. He had heard the swish of the curtain on its rail.

Jacina closed the curtain immediately. "I..I am sorry, my Lord. I came in to borrow a b..book. I did not know you were here. I will leave this instant."

"No, no! No, Jacina, I am growing weary of my own company. Stay."

Jacina moved to the chair opposite the Earl and sat down. "Why do you want the curtains drawn, my Lord, when..."

"When I cannot see?" finished the Earl. He frowned. "My mood is such that I prefer at the moment to think of the library in darkness. There! Does that satisfy your curiosity?"

"I..I think so, my Lord."

"Since you are here, we cannot have you idle. Why not read to me? You will find some Wordsworth on a shelf over there."

Jacina was delighted to obey the Earl. She took down the leather bound book and began to read.

Two verses in there was a knock at the door. "The deuce!" swore the Earl softly.

Jarrold entered. "A letter, my Lord," he said.

"Where is it from, Jarrold?" asked the Earl.

"It has a Swiss postmark, my Lord."

The Earl sat up. "Switzerland! I had not expected her to write so soon. I must know what is in it. Jacina, read it to me quickly."

Jarrold delivered the letter into Jacina's trembling hands. He bowed and left. The Earl drummed his fingers on the arms of his chair.

Jacina's pulse raced. She did not want this painful task. Why could the Earl not ask his secretary or even his valet to read the letter to him? Did he not realise what torture he was inflicting on her with this command? The protest died on her lips as she looked at the Earl and saw his intense anticipation. Of course he did not know what he was asking of her. He had no idea of what she felt for him.

Jacina opened the letter. The words seemed to burn on her tongue as she spoke.

"My dear husband, I have arrived at the Hotel Cronos in St Moritz. Please join me here. I have found a chateau to rent. Tomorrow I will go and start preparing it for us. It is beautifully situated on a lake. There we will be able to put right a marriage that began so badly. It will be a true honeymoon. No other woman in the w..world can love you as I...do. I long for you."

Jacina's flesh was on fire as she read out these last words. They could have come from her own heart, her own lips. Her voice faltered and she could not go on.

"I...I'm sorry.." she whispered. "I...need some... water."

She almost knocked over the decanter on the table beside her. She poured herself a glass and lifted it with trembling hands. She drank in great gulps.

The Earl sat immobile, his eyes seeming to stare into space. "I did not expect such words," he said at last.

He rang the bell at his elbow and his valet hurried in. Curtly the Earl told him to start packing. They were travelling tomorrow.

"To – Switzerland?" asked the valet.

"That's right," said the Earl. "To Switzerland. To be reunited with my wife."

*

The Earl set off early at dawn with his valet. Jacina did not even hear him leave.

Her misery was acute. *'It will be a true honeymoon'.* She was only too well aware that now at last the Earl and Felice would have the opportunity to truly become man and wife.

She had not taken a book from the library the day before and so she decided to go and get one today. She had to distract herself somehow until her father arrived.

She found the curtains in the library still drawn. She pulled them open and looked out at the drear November skies. Then she turned and surveyed the room. Her eye immediately alighted on the letter from Felice. It lay crumpled on the side table. She remembered that she had left it there, but she most certainly had not crumpled it up like that! As she gazed on it a frown started to crease her brow. She went over and picked up the letter. She stared hard at it, biting her lip. Then with a sudden exclamation she turned on her heels and raced from the room. Within moments she was in the nursery.

"Sarah, Sarah!"

Sarah had taken a chill and was sitting by the fire, wrapped in a blanket. She blinked at Jacina. "What is it, my dear?"

"That letter Felice Delisle sent you...when she was engaged to Crispian...do you still have it?"

Sarah seemed befuddled. "Why, no. I burned it."

"You *burned* it?"

Sarah set her lips. "I didn't want to keep no letter from

104

her any longer. Not after all that happened."

Jacina sank onto a chair in dismay.

A moment ago, in the library, that old letter to Sarah had suddenly flashed into her mind. She had remembered that when she first saw it, she had been struck by its *dainty handwriting*.

The writing in the letter she had read to the Earl was completely different – large and looped and *not dainty at all*.

The Felice who wrote that letter to Sarah and the Felice who wrote yesterday to the Earl, *could not possibly be the same person*.

The Earl would not have realised the handwriting was not the handwriting of the fiancée with whom he had once corresponded *because he was blind*. Apart from the Earl, there was no-one else left at Castle Ruven who knew what Felice's handwriting should look like. The old Earl was dead and Crispian was dead. Even so, Jacina suddenly thought, Felice and Fronard had taken no chances. Nancy had seen them burn the letters Crispian had received from his fiancée. No doubt they had also burned any letters to the old Earl or to Hugo when he was in India in case anybody found them.

That was what Fronard was doing all that time he was 'snooping' about the castle. Eliminating any tell tale traces of Felice Delisle. The *real* Felice Delisle. They never imagined Felice being kind enough to have written to her fiancé's old nanny.

Jacina's heart thudded with horror. If the woman who had married the Earl ten days ago was not the real Felice, then who was she? Who was she and who was Fronard and *what did they want*?

They wanted...they wanted the rubies and the emeralds and the Ruven diamonds that had come to the so-called

Felice on her marriage to the Earl! *But was that all?* Why had Felice enticed the Earl to Switzerland when she already had all the jewels in her possession? Jacina racked her brains. What more did they want, what more?

Suddenly she sat up straight. Of course! Her father had explained it all that day in the library when he was discussing the old Earl's will. The estate was entailed. Felice would never inherit. It would go to either the Earl's eldest child or, should he die without issue, to a distant male relative. So in recompense the old Earl had settled a 'generous sum' on Felice, which she would receive *should her husband die before her*.

Felice and Fronard wanted that money and they could only get it if Hugo, Earl of Ruven was dead.

They must have plotted to kill him at some point and make it look like an accident. Jacina felt the blood drain from her face.

No wonder Fronard had accepted the challenge to a duel with such alacrity. No wonder 'Felice' had collapsed in hysterical laughter. The Earl and Jacina had smoothed the way for them. They could get rid of the Earl and *no-one would suspect that was what they had planned all along*.

It was horrifyingly clear to Jacina. When the Earl was brought back alive to the castle that day Felice had had to think very quickly. She had acted the part of the devoted wife to perfection and the Earl had forgiven her. She was back in his favour and she had confidently left for Switzerland to put the finishing touches to her plan. To find a chateau where she could isolate the Earl and then, with Fronard's help...dispose of him.

If her recent exemplary behaviour had not fully convinced her husband to follow her, then that last letter would!

Jacina was wondering what Felice planned to do with the valet, when she became aware that Sarah was speaking to her.

"If I'd have known you wanted that letter I'd never have burned it."

"That's alright, Sarah. Don't worry about it."

Sarah coughed and drew her chair nearer the fire.

Jacina moaned softly as she thought of her predicament.

The Earl's life was in danger but who would believe her, who? The one piece of evidence – the letter to Sarah, which could have been compared with the recent letter to the Earl – was gone. Sarah would believe her, but she could not involve Sarah in yet another series of allegations, particularly as the old lady was not well.

Her father would surely listen but he might not arrive for another day or two. That would be too late! If Fronard had not already met Felice en route, he would surely be waiting for her in Switzerland. The Earl was travelling straight into a trap.

It struck Jacina that Felice had waited to leave until she was sure Doctor Carlton was coming to fetch his daughter home, before she had allowed herself to leave Castle Ruven. Was that because Felice suspected Jacina might yet plant doubts about his wife in the Earl's mind?

Jacina rose to her feet and began to pace the room. There was no time to lose. Someone had to make the journey to Switzerland to warn the Earl. Who could she send?

She stopped before Sarah's dressing table and stared at herself in the mirror. Her eyes looked haunted and her face was white. Even as she looked, she knew there was only one person who might be able to convince the Earl his life was in danger. Herself!

She, who had never left the environs of Ruvensford, must set out alone for Switzerland.

And she must set out that very night!

CHAPTER EIGHT

The lights of the Hotel Cronos looked warm and inviting from where Jacina stood on the pavement opposite. She had just alighted from the fiacre that had met her carriage from Geneva. The vehicle had been draughty and Jacina had shivered all the way. She had barely eaten in two days – just some fruit and a brioche snatched at a baker's stall in Paris.

It had been a long, cold journey from England and she hoped she would never make another like it. She had never felt so alone in her life.

Only the stable boy, whom she had bribed to drive her to the station in Carlisle, knew she was leaving. She had left a letter to wait for her father. All she had taken with her was the money her father had left her and a small travelling case.

If it were not for the thought of the Earl and the danger he was in, she would have turned back more than once.

She hoped she was not too late. When she had arrived at Carlisle station that night, it was only to discover that there was no train until the following morning. So she was arriving here in St. Moritz a whole day later than the Earl.

With trepidation Jacina picked up her travelling case and crossed the street to the hotel.

The concierge regarded her suspiciously when she asked if the Earl of Ruven was alone. She explained that she was a friend from England with important news and at last the concierge instructed a maid to show her up to the Earl's room. The Countess, the concierge added, had gone out early that morning and had not returned.

Jacina rapped at the Earl's door with a pounding heart. The door opened and there at last he stood, the man for whom she had dared this long journey.

"Jacina!" he exclaimed.

All her remaining strength deserted her in one go. With a cry she collapsed unconscious into his arms.

When she opened her eyes a few moments later she was lying on a chaise long. She struggled upright in alarm. "My..my Lord?"

His voice reassured her from nearby. "I am here, Jacina." He was sitting at a writing desk, the chair swivelled her way.

She stared at him, her thoughts in a whirl. "M..my Lord. When you opened the door you...you said my name before I spoke. How...how did you know....?"

"That it was you?" The Earl stood and held out his hand. "Come here, Jacina."

Jacina rose unsteadily and moved towards the Earl. He took her hand and led her in front of an ornate mirror that hung on the wall. She could see her own reflection and that of the Earl behind her. Slowly the Earl raised a candle until he was holding it close to his eyes. His dark, liquid gaze arrested her attention. She gazed back for a moment and then gasped.

"You...you can see!"

"Yes, Jacina. I can see."

When he had regained consciousness after the duel, he had soon realised that his sight was returning. At first he saw only blurred and shadowy outlines. It was only gradually that the world came into sharper focus.

"Your father believed I had suffered a 'trauma blindness'," said the Earl. "It turns out he was right!"

Jacina was dizzy with joy, but she could not help wondering why he had kept the fact that he was beginning to see again hidden from everybody.

He said that he did not want to raise false hopes, including his own, until he could be sure his sight had returned for good. There were other reasons for remaining silent, but first he wanted to know how and why Jacina had travelled all the way to Switzerland on her own.

Jacina noticed that as he spoke, his eyes seemed to be devouring her image in the mirror. She blushed and lowered her gaze. The Earl excused himself. "I am sorry for staring so, Jacina. I am just re-acquainting myself with the pretty girl whose bonnet fell into the river. Come, come and sit down and tell me your story."

He listened keenly to what Jacina had to tell him. At the end he turned his face away to hide his emotion.

"You have risked so much for me, my little friend," he said.

He went to a cabinet and took out a bottle of brandy. He poured a glass for himself and Jacina. Then he proceeded to tell her that the other reason he had decided to pretend to be still blind was to be better able to see. When Jacina looked puzzled, the Earl explained that when he had first opened his eyes and realised his vision was returning, Felice happened to be in the room. He saw that she was pacing the floor with boredom, now and then throwing a glance of such dislike in his direction, that he immediately knew her 'conversion' to the perfect and devoted wife was no more than an act.

"She realised I was awake and came to the bedside," said the Earl. "She leaned over me and spoke in honeyed tones, but her eyes were full of resentment. She even clenched her fists as she gazed on me."

He had no doubt then that she wished him ill and was putting on a performance so as to lull him into a false sense of security. He suspected that she had some ulterior motive and he decided to remain 'blind' until he knew what it was. That was why he had kept his chamber and the library so dark – so that people could not see him so clearly.

When the Countess suggested the trip to Switzerland he began to guess her plan. The letter that he asked Jacina to read aloud in the library fuelled his suspicions. He knew full well that his wife did not 'long' for him at all. After Jacina left the library he had tried to read the letter himself. His sight was still not keen enough for him to make out all the words, but he noticed the large signature and recognised immediately that it was not that of the real Felice.

He searched for the letters he had received from his fiancée when he was in India, but they had disappeared. He realised that Fronard or the imposter Felice must have found them and destroyed them. It left him with no proof with which to confront the Countess and he decided that he must continue to play along with her to see what would transpire. It was clear that whatever happened, he must travel to Switzerland to find the real Felice.

The only person who knew he was no longer blind – apart from Jacina herself – was his valet and he had told him once they were both en route to Switzerland.

"My apparent helplessness is my trump card" said the Earl. "It makes Fronard and the Countess...careless. Already

I have seen Fronard."

"You...you have seen Fronard?"

"Yes. He had the impertinence to sit near us at dinner. I knew it was him by the way he was grinning like a jackass at the Countess, believing I was totally unaware."

Jacina thought the Earl was very brave to be so sanguine in the face of danger.

"What will you do now?" she asked.

"I must find the real Felice. Once I have found her, their game is up. Until then I have nothing to prove that the Countess is not who she says she is. Until then I am still married to – to a woman whose true identity I do not know."

"She is v..very beautiful, though, isn't she?" ventured Jacina.

"Oh yes," breathed the Earl. "Very beautiful indeed."

Jacina hung her head. The Earl had been in the hotel a full night with the Countess. She could not but wonder if they had spent that night together. The Countess was beautiful and determined. The Earl had appetite like other men. Why should he not have succumbed, even for one night, to her undoubted charms?

The Earl was brooding. "You are a sweet fool indeed to come all this way to warn me. But as you see, I needed no warning. I knew it all."

Tired and emotional, Jacina burst into tears. "Oh, please do not say it was a waste of time. I have travelled for over two days without stopping. I was so frightened by the noise and bustle in London...and the sea was so rough I was sick...and I got lost in Paris finding my way to the coach...and it was so cold travelling over the mountains! Oh do not say it was all for nothing, for upon my soul I could not bear it."

The Earl reached for her and held her sobbing at his breast. She turned her tear stained face up to him and with a moan he leant to kiss her wet cheek. The room seemed to whirl about her. She felt herself melting in his embrace, yielding to his hungry lips...

Then, as suddenly as he had reached for her, the Earl pushed her from him and leapt groaning to his feet. "No, no – it cannot be! In the eyes of the world I am still a married man. And even when I unmask this imposter, remember I will still not be free. I will still be engaged to the real Felice. Remember that and help me – my dear Jacina – my oh so pretty little friend."

He went to the cabinet and poured himself another glass of brandy. Jacina watched him in a daze. His kiss had exhilarated her...his words had infused her like fire and ice. She did not know what to think or what to do.

There was a rap at the door and someone rattled the door handle. Swiftly the Earl pulled Jacina to her feet and thrust her behind a screen in the corner of the room. He went to the door – which he had taken the precaution of locking after Jacina's arrival – and turned the key to open it.

Through the latticework of the screen, Jacina saw the Countess sail into the room, flinging her shawl onto the chaise as she passed.

"Why did you lock the door, mon cher?"

"How would I have known – if someone undesirable had entered?

The Countess put her arms around the Earl's neck and kissed him. "Am I what you call – undesirable?' she said. Her tone was teasing but Jacina saw that her eyes were hard and bright as she surveyed the Earl.

Jacina marvelled at how still the Earl held his gaze, staring over the Countess's head as if still blind. "No. You are not undesirable, my dear."

"My darling!" the Countess pressed closer to the Earl. "I have come to tell you ze chateau is nearly ready. I return there tonight. Tomorrow I will finish ze preparations so it is perfect for you. And zen you come in ze evening, hein?"

"I have heard there are bandits in the mountains," said the Earl with an innocent expression. "Would it not be better to travel during the day? It would not do for my valet and me to be – ambushed and killed, would it?"

The Countess pulled away from him and flounced to the mirror. "Bandits? Zis is just a story. You will be safe." She stood patting a few hairs back into place under her hat. "I do not see why you need zis valet at all," she added casually. "I will look after you so well. Why don't you send him back to England?"

"I should prefer to keep him with me, my dear. He is familiar with my – needs."

"But my darling," the Countess turned and advanced on the Earl, her voice dripping honey. "When we are at ze chateau – remember – that is when we can become truly man and wife."

Despite herself, Jacina closed her eyes in relief as she realised that the Earl had remained aloof from the Countess' charms.

"Just imagine," the Countess was continuing. "Ze fires will be lit and ze supper ready. It will be so beautiful – ze two of us – alone. Why not leave your valet behind just for a day or two, hein?"

The Earl appeared to weaken. "I will consider it," he said.

The Countess bit her lip in frustration. Then, obviously deciding to leave the question of the valet to be dealt with some other way, she reached up and traced a finger over the Earl's lip. Her voice took on a low and seductive tone.

"I ache to have you in my bed," she murmured. "I have waited so long for you."

The Earl clenched his jaw. "And I – for you – my dear."

Felice gave a quick smile to herself and stepped away. She picked up her shawl and moved to the door. "Zen we will meet – tomorrow – at ze chateau!"

"By all means," said the Earl.

No sooner had the door closed behind the Countess than Jacina rushed out from her hiding place. "Please m..my Lord, I beg you, do not go to the chateau. Fronard will be there and...your life will be in danger."

"Do not worry, Jacina," said the Earl gently. "I have no intention of going. Tomorrow my valet and I are setting out for Rougemont."

"Rougemont?"

"A village high in the alps. The headmistress of the school Felice attended in Geneva retired there. Felice went to live with her after she had recuperated from her illness. If Felice is anywhere, she is there. Though I do not know why I have not heard from her."

"Perhaps...your letters to her...or hers to you, were intercepted somehow by the Countess."

"Yes. That is possible. Anyway, now I must think of what to do with you."

The Earl decided to entrust the valet with the task of finding a room for Jacina in the hotel, a room as far away as possible from prying eyes and wagging tongues. She must keep out of sight, for the Earl was sure her own life would be in danger, if Fronard and the Countess knew she was here.

Tomorrow she must return to England.

"Please do not make me, m..my Lord. I want to stay...here with you."

The Earl looked troubled. "Jacina, I cannot allow that. Imagine if something happened to you! I could never forgive myself."

The Earl sent for the valet and gave his instructions. The valet was astonished to see Jacina but went off without a word and returned shortly with a key. Reluctantly Jacina followed him to a little room hidden high in the eaves of the hotel.

Later he brought her a supper of mutton stew. Jacina had earlier felt weak with hunger, but now she had lost her appetite. After a few bites she pushed the tray away. She washed her face and hands in the bowl provided and then slipped under the huge feather-filled quilt on the bed. She had barely laid her head on the pillow when she heard shouts and oaths from the street. There was the sound of scuffling and a loud cry of pain. She leapt up and rushed to the tiny window.

A figure sat groaning on the cobbles below. A short, stout pole lay in the gutter where it had been thrown. Running footsteps receded up the street. What should she do? The Earl had told her to keep out of sight but how could she leave someone lying out there injured in the cold night?

She threw on her cloak and went into the corridor. She was immediately aware that other doors on the landing below were opening. She moved stealthily down the stairs and listened. She heard the voice of the concierge reassuring guests as he came up the stairs. Then she heard him knock at the Earl's door. He spoke to the Earl in a low voice. The Earl sounded anxious as he replied. "Have him carried to my room," he ordered. "And send for a doctor."

The concierge went back down to the lobby. The Earl waited, leaning over the balustrade. Jacina crept down the stairs to his side.

"What has happened?" she asked.

"My valet was attacked as he returned to the hotel from a nearby tavern," said the Earl grimly. "The assailant broke one of his legs with a pole."

Jacina was shocked. "Who could have done such a thing?"

The Earl glanced at her. "Who else but Fronard? This will ensure that, whether I wished it or not, my valet could not travel with me tomorrow to the chateau. Fronard is convinced I will still go, because the Countess is expecting me."

Jacina shook her head. "They are so...so evil, my Lord. But what will you do now about Rougemont. Will you still go there...alone?"

"I will and must," replied the Earl. "The valet will be comfortable in my room until I return." He saw that Jacina was shivering and gently drew her cloak more closely around her. "Go back to bed, Jacina. I will deal with everything."

"But m..my Lord..."

"Jacina!" The Earl's voice was suddenly sharp. "I command you to do as I say!"

Reluctantly Jacina climbed the narrow stairs to her little room.

She could not sleep however. She heard the heavy knocker on the hotel door announce the arrival of the doctor. She heard the footsteps hurrying up and down the stairs as the valet was attended to. She heard the church bells toll. She heard the first cock crow and saw the first slivers of light in the sky.

Every time she closed her eyes she saw the Earl's face as he bent to kiss her. She remembered the way his lips lingered on hers in a way that suggested he felt more for her than mere friendship.

She tossed and turned and then threw back the quilt. If she could not sleep there was no point remaining in bed.

She got out of bed and went to the wash-stand. She poured some water from the jug into the pewter basin and slipped her night gown from her shoulders to wash. She leaned forward to splash her face and as she rose met her own reflection in the wash-stand mirror. Her shoulders looked white as porcelain with a faint flush under the skin. Her cheeks were flushed too and her eyes bright. She thought with faint excitement that there in the mirror was the girl the Earl had called his 'dear Jacina,' his 'oh so pretty little friend'.

She buried her face in her hands. She must stop this. She could not let herself imagine that the Earl's heart beat as wildly for her as her heart beat for him. He was not free now and never would be. When this matter with Fronard and the Countess was resolved, he was still committed to the real Felice. He had reminded Jacina of that and had asked her to help him. More than anything else, the Earl needed her as a friend.

She lifted her head as she heard the wheels of a carriage rattling on the cobbles. This must be the carriage that would bear the Earl away to Rougemont. If she left for England today, who knew when she would ever see him again? He had asked for her help and friendship. Then that was what she would give him.

She washed and dressed hurriedly and was in the hotel lobby as the Earl himself descended. He was taken aback when he saw her.

"I do not think there is transport to Geneva this early," he said.

"I am not going to Geneva, m..my Lord. I am going with you."

The Earl's brow darkened. "I cannot agree to this, Jacina. I do not want to have to worry about your safety as well as everything else."

"But neither Monsieur Fronard nor the Countess know where you are going, do they?"

"No," the Earl admitted. "They do not."

"In fact, they will be waiting at the chateau for you to arrive tonight, won't they?"

The Earl nodded reluctantly. "They will."

"So!" cried Jacina triumphantly. "What danger can there be if I come along?"

The Earl sighed and shook his head. "Jacina, I – "

"When you find the real Felice," persisted Jacina. "Think of the tale you will be bringing her. She will find it incredible! Would it not be better if there was a friend with you...who could corroborate your story?" The Earl considered this. "Perhaps you are right – " he said slowly.

"I am! I know I am, my...my Lord," cried Jacina happily.

A flicker of a smile hovered on the Earl's lips as he regarded her. "Well, my little friend – you will need warmer garments than those if you are coming with me. I will ask the concierge if his wife can lend you something."

Half an hour later Jacina was ensconced in the carriage with the Earl. She knew she looked strange with a woollen cloak that was too big for her, a worsted skirt, a fur hat and a muff the size of a cat, but she did not care.

The Earl had been amused at her attire when she

appeared outside the hotel, but he had been careful not to show it. The coachman must believe the Earl was blind, for he might gossip at stops along the way and word could then travel back to St Moritz.

"I would not want Fronard and my wife alerted to the fact that I am not quite as helpless as they think," reflected the Earl. "Not yet, anyway."

The air was sharp as they set out. A cold mist hung over the roofs. Jacina looked at the streets through which they passed with interest. The houses had steep gables and balconies and were brightly painted. The cobbles of the roadway looked scrubbed and clean.

The Earl told her about his valet. The valet had not seen the face of the man who attacked him as the man had been wearing a hooded cloak. He had stepped out suddenly from an alleyway at the side of the hotel. There was nobody about as it was past midnight.

The valet was in great pain but bore it stoically. He said it was his own fault for staying so long in the tavern. He had slipped out without the Earl's permission to explore the town. The doctor who examined the valet said the leg would heal in time but he must not walk on it for two months.

"I do not think he will be too heart-sore at having to stay in St. Moritz for a while," mused the Earl. "It seems he met a very pretty Swiss miss last night!"

At the edge of the town the Earl asked the coachman to stop, so he and Jacina could take some refreshment at a small hostelry that was just opening its doors. There had been no-one about at the Hotel Cronos that morning to serve breakfast.

They were shown to a little table covered with a red check tablecloth. Jacina had not eaten properly for days and she hungrily devoured the warm bread and honey and gulped down a bowl of frothy hot milk.

The Earl did everything as if he could not see. Jacina marvelled at his powers of self control.

The mist was clearing by the time they left.

The coachman was smoking a pipe up on his box. He nodded amiably as they approached and knocked his pipe out on the roof of the coach. The Earl helped Jacina in and she felt herself shudder at the touch of his hand. Before he settled himself on the seat opposite, the Earl drew a rug over her knees. Then the coach set off again.

If only our errand was not so portentous, thought Jacina, I could imagine that we were simply travellers, exploring a strange country together.

The Earl tapped her arm and pointed out of the window. Jacina looked out and gasped. There were the Bernese Alps, great glittering forms with heads of ice.

Somewhere up there lay the truth about the real Felice Delisle.

CHAPTER NINE

The road wound higher and higher into the mountains. Sometimes it ran through thick forest of pine, where all that could be heard was the grind of the carriage wheels and the tramp of the horses' hooves. Sometimes it crossed stone bridges where all that could be seen below, far below, was a swift ribbon of water. More often it clung to the side of sheer rock, with nothing but a dizzying chasm for Jacina to look out on.

Now and then the horses slipped on the hard, icy road and for a terrifying moment the coach would begin to slide backwards. Then the coachman would crack his whip and cry 'hoi hoi hoi'. The horses would strain harder in their harness and the coach would move on.

The air grew sharper and colder. Jacina was glad of the heavy cloak, unflattering as it might be. She thrust her hands deep in the huge muff.

She was always aware of the presence of the Earl.

Whenever she glanced his way his features were set and stern. His dark eyes brooded under their heavy lids. He hardly spoke, though should Jacina ask him a question, he always answered her with courtesy.

She felt that as the coach rose into the mountains and into the world of Felice, the Earl's thoughts lingered more and more on the fiancée he was going to meet for the first time.

She could not help wondering if the real Felice was pretty. The Earl's brother Crispian had fallen in love with her, she thought wryly. Why should not the Earl himself?

Then she would pinch her own hand sharply inside the muff. This would never do. She had come along as the Earl's friend and that was how she must behave and think.

At noon the coachman drew up at a tiny hostelry. The patron came out with flagons of Swiss beer and hunks of bread and cheese. Jacina asked timidly if she might have soup instead of beer. The Earl smiled and instructed the patron to bring his guest some potato soup.

After this refreshment they continued on their way. Jacina closed her eyes and in a second was asleep.

When she awoke some two hours later, she could feel that the rug had been drawn up over her shoulders to keep her warm. She opened her eyes and looked straight into those of the Earl. She blushed as she wondered if he had been watching her sleep.

The Earl turned his eyes quickly away. "It's snowing," he said.

Jacina looked out of the carriage window. Huge, dazzlingly white flakes danced in the air.

The road grew steeper. The coach seemed to be almost vertical as it climbed. Then the road levelled out and ran through forest again. As dusk fell, Jacina began to hear the howl of wolves from amidst the trees.

It was dark when the coach rolled into the small town of Savrin. The coachman pulled up in front of the one hotel, which stood opposite the town hall.

A porter hurried out to take their bags. He led them into the hotel while the coachman drove the coach and horses into the stable yard.

The Earl ordered two rooms. The coachman would sleep on the settle in the hotel parlour.

Jacina was glad to be able to refresh herself in her room. She noticed that her skin was glowing from the fresh mountain air. She brushed her hair and changed from her boots into a pair of satin slippers. Then she went down to join the Earl for dinner.

A white tiled stove kept the dining room warm. There were two long wooden tables and benches. Some customers were gathered near the stove chatting and drinking tankards of beer.

Jacina sat with the Earl on one of the benches.

The patron bustled up to introduce himself and take their orders. He said there was a tasty rabbit stew on the menu. Jacina said she would be happy with that and the Earl ordered two bowls.

The patron was curious about the blind Earl and his companion. Once he had delivered the order to the kitchen, he returned and hovered at their table. He asked them where they were going.

The Earl hesitated and then said, "Rougemont."

There was an immediate silence in the room. The customers around the stove stopped their chatter. The patron stroked his chin.

"How long since you were last there?" he asked.

"I have never been there," said the Earl.

"Well, if you had, you'd find it much changed."

The Earl asked him why and the patron explained.

"There was an avalanche there this year. A quarter of the village was destroyed, Monsieur. Many people died."

The Earl sat very still. "When was this exactly?"

Jacina looked on anxiously as the patron wrinkled his brow. "Late March or thereabouts," he replied.

The Earl drew in his breath. "A month after the old Earl died," he said softly.

"Pardon, Monsieur?" said the patron.

The Earl shook his head. "It is not important. Tell me, do you know anything about the headmistress from Geneva who retired there?"

The patron said he did not, but one of the customers by the stove spoke up. "She was killed, Monsieur. So were other people in the household. Two young women who lived with her were brought out alive. One of them died later though."

Jacina glanced at the Earl. She could not read his features.

"Tell me," said the Earl. "How long will it take to get to Rougemont from here?" The patron explained that it would not be possible to take the coach all the way. The road was only wide enough for a coach and four until it reached the Saultier Pass. After that, there was only a track into the valley of Rougemont. The Earl would need a packhorse.

The Earl decided that they would hire a packhorse from the hotel tomorrow. They would tie the horse to the back of the coach. When they reached the Saultier Pass, the Earl and Jacina would continue their journey on the packhorse while the coach returned to Savrin.

The rabbit stew then arrived and all conversation ceased. The Earl and Jacina ate quickly and retired to their rooms.

That night, Jacina dreamt of a towering wave of snow bearing down on her out of the mountains.

*

It was twenty miles from Savrin to the Saultier Pass. The horses' hooves crunched through the powdery snow. The Earl sat silent the whole way. Jacina looked out at the breath-taking scenery. The mountains towered above her. The sky was the colour of a clear pearl.

The landscape was so beautiful that it set Jacina thinking. Perhaps there were other reasons why Felice had not wished to go to Castle Ruven after the death of her fiancé, Crispian. Perhaps here in these mountains she was able to find an inner peace that she feared might be denied her in England and with people that she did not know.

At the Saultier pass the coach halted. The road did indeed peter out here. Ahead lay a snowy track that disappeared into a ravine.

The coachman untied the packhorse from the back of the coach. The Earl lifted Jacina into the saddle. Then he mounted behind her. "From now on I think it is safe for me to be no longer blind," he whispered.

"I shall be glad of that," smiled Jacina.

The coachman turned the coach. He called out 'au revoir' and set off back to Savrin.

The Earl and Jacina were alone in what seemed like an endless wilderness.

A wind began to whistle about them, as they rode down into the ravine. The rocks rose sheer and dark on either side.

The ravine path was rocky and the horse stumbled in places, but Jacina always felt secure with the Earl's strong arms about her.

They passed a frozen waterfall. It looked like a mirror hung in mid-air.

After an hour's ride the ravine widened out into a valley. Snow must have fallen heavily here last night. The whole valley was under a pristine, shining coat of white. In the distance, Jacina made out a huddle of red roofs around a steeple.

In leaving the ravine they also left behind the cold wind. Jacina threw back the hood of her cloak, the better to feel the bracing air on her face.

The Earl's arms seemed to tighten around her. She felt his warm breath on her neck.

If only they could travel like this for eternity, thought Jacina. She felt neither hunger nor thirst nor fatigue. Her blood beat with the thrill of feeling the Earl so close to her.

Rougemont was silent when they reached it. They rode into a deserted village square. Looking about them, the Earl and Jacina noticed that four streets led off the square. One street ended abruptly in a wall of snow-covered debris that rose to a height of twenty feet or so. Here and there the peak of a gable thrust through. Otherwise the surface was unbroken.

They sat sombrely for a moment, transfixed by this ominous sight. Then the Earl quickly dismounted. He extended his arms and Jacina slid from the horse's back. For one second, the Earl seemed to clasp her to him as though he would never let go. Then he stood back. He did not meet her eye, but looked about him.

A small boy in lederhosen had appeared in the square. The Earl beckoned to him. The boy approached warily at first, but his pace quickened when the Earl took out some coins. The boy promised to see to it that the horse was fed and watered. When the Earl asked whom he might approach for information, the boy gestured towards a large house with red painted shutters that stood on the other side of the square.

"Ma grand-mere!" he said gravely. "Elle connaît tout."

The Earl gave a slight smile.

"Well," he said to Jacina. "Let us see if his grandmother does indeed know everything!"

They crossed the square to the house with red shutters and the Earl raised the knocker on the front door. The knock seemed to resound through the whole village. Jacina sensed faces peering from windows all around.

Slow, shuffling steps could be heard on the other side of the door. The door creaked open and a bent, wan little old woman stood before them.

"Oui? Que voulez-vous?"

The Earl gave a bow. "Madame, we are seeking – nous cherchons – Mademoiselle Felice Delisle."

At this, a shudder seemed to run through the old woman. She closed her eyes and gave a sigh. Then, trembling, she raised a claw like finger and pointed in the direction of the steeple that Jacina had spied from afar.

"La petite est là," she said, and closed the door.

The Earl had paled as he followed the direction of the old woman's pointing finger.

He strode off without another word. Jacina hurried bleakly in his wake. The Earl seemed to have forgotten her completely. It was as if he were hurrying to some assignation, the import of which was a secret harboured only in his own heart.

She was aware of faces watching from half open doors as they passed by. At the end of the street the Earl turned a corner. Jacina ran to catch up. She saw the Earl open the wicket gate of the churchyard and pass through.

Her heart flew against her breastbone like a bird beating itself against glass.

Was it here, in this churchyard, in this icy earth, that the Earl would finally find his Felice?

She followed his progress amongst the headstones with her eyes. She saw him stop short at one grave, stare, and move slowly on to the next. Here he staggered for a moment and then steadied himself to stay, his head lowered, his shoulders sagging as if under some sudden unbearable burden.

Jacina slowly followed his track through the churchyard.

She glanced at the first headstone that had arrested him. It read

Madame Hermione Gravalt,
née en Genevre Avril 10 1810
Mort en Rougemont Mars 25 1857

She knew this must be the headmistress with whom Felice had lived.

The words on the second tomb seemed to leap at her darkly from the stone.

Felice Delisle
Née en Genevre Novembre 12 1836
Mort en Rougemont Juin 1857

Felice Delisle had died in June, three months after the avalanche.

Tears sprang to Jacina's eyes, though whether for the Earl, herself or Felice she was not certain. All she was aware of, was this stark tomb under a lowering sky, and the Earl, seemingly crushed at the loss of his fiancée.

At last the Earl stirred. He lifted his head and started at the sight of Jacina, as if only just aware that she was beside him.

"It ends here," he said simply. "The life – of my brother Crispian – ends here." He gave a heavy sigh. "I always felt that in honouring his choice of wife, I honoured his memory. I felt I could keep something of him alive in this world. Now it is over."

Jacina bowed her head. "I am...so sorry...my Lord."

"I do not mourn a woman I loved," murmured the Earl, "for I never knew her. I mourn the woman my brother loved. For my brother's sake, I wished to make her happy. Now that can never be."

Jacina clasped her hands together and said nothing.

The Earl drew a deep breath and straightened. "Though Felice is dead," he said, "the story is not yet ended. We must now discover the identity of the woman who calls herself my wife. My suspicions are that she also came from this village."

"Perhaps we should try the parish priest," suggested Jacina.

The Earl thought this was a good idea. He and Jacina soon found the priest's house. It stood opposite the church and had green shutters and a bell at the door. A maid showed them into a study where a cheerful fire burned. The priest entered soon after. He was grave and stooped. He introduced himself, in excellent English, as Father Lamont and welcomed them to Rougemont.

"Though alas," he added mournfully, "you come to a village that has lost its heart. A village in shock. You have heard, I suppose, of the tragedy that befell us?"

"I have," said the Earl soberly. "Indeed, I have been personally touched by it, for I lost a young woman whom I held in great esteem. Her name was Felice Delisle."

"Ah! Mademoiselle Felice!" The priest looked at him sadly. "I knew her, Monsieur. She was a gentle, pious soul.

I am so glad that at last someone has come to pay their respects."

The Earl frowned. "I would have come before," he said, "had I known. Why was my family not informed?"

Father Lamont's sighed. "You were not informed? I see. I see. Well, there is much to be explained. You must understand, Monsieur, there were – certain anomalies – after her death. I will tell you all. But first, let me ring for some tea."

At the sound of the bell the maid came in. The priest ordered tea and then sat back in his chair, the tips of his fingers together under his chin.

"Spare me no details," said the Earl quickly. "I want to know everything. Begin please with the avalanche."

The priest's eyes took on a stricken look. "Oh Monsieur – how can I describe such a night? How can I describe a vision of hell? The mountain roared and rushed down upon us. It came in a tumult of rock and ice and snow. Many villagers were killed, many injured. Twenty dwellings were destroyed. One of those was the house of Madame Gravalt."

The Earl nodded. "In Savrin," he said softly, "I was told that two young women were rescued alive from that house."

"That is right," murmured the priest. "Mademoiselle Felice and another young woman. How they survived is almost a miracle, Monsieur. Everyone else in that house died. Madame Gravalt – Madame Frouleau, an elderly teacher who was lodging with her – their maid." The priest paused and shook his head. "The two young women were alive, but Mademoiselle Felice was badly injured. She lay in a coma for many weeks. The doctor did all he could to save her, but God's will was stronger."

The Earl bowed his head. "She never regained consciousness?"

"No, Monsieur."

The Earl rose from his seat and went to the window. He stood with his hands clasped behind his back, his eyes fixed on the mountain that loomed over the village.

"Who was – the other young woman?" he asked.

"The other young woman," Father Lamont echoed in an unhappy tone. "She, Monsieur, is a large part of the story I have to tell you. When Madame Gravalt was running the school in Geneva she was kind enough to take in her orphaned niece. The name of this niece was Lisette. Lisette and Mademoiselle Felice were – polar opposites, do you say? Mademoiselle Felice was so quiet, she loved books, study, prayer. She had a delicate constitution. This Lisette was – well, she was different. She made her aunt's life a misery. Yet such is the mystery of God's plan, that it was Lisette who survived that terrible night and not Felice."

"Were she and Felice friends?" asked the Earl.

The priest considered. "In Geneva, I don't know for sure. But when Madame Gravalt retired to Rougemont her niece came with her. Felice joined them after her illness – and certainly then the two girls were thrown very much into each other's company. Monsieur, we villagers mourned the loss of Felice very much. She was what we call 'tres sympathique.' Whereas Lisette – "

He paused as the maid came in with the tea. As she set out the cups he gently asked her something. The maid frowned and said, "elle avait une ame très cruelle!"

"There you have it," said Father Lamont. "Lucille was a friend of Madame Gravalt's maid, the one who died. 'A very cruel soul' is how her friend used to describe Lisette. I would not go so far as that – but she was certainly –

troubled."

He paused to take a cup of tea from Lucille and then he continued.

"You know, Madame Gravalt was not running a charity school. Her niece was expected to work for her keep. This did not suit such a girl as Lisette Gravalt. She wanted more in life. In Geneva she took a lover. This lover was the son of a local magistrate but his father had thrown him out of the family home because of his gambling. He was a bad influence on Lisette. She would sneak out at night, join him in taverns and gambling dens. She and her lover planned to elope. Madame Gravalt discovered their intentions and put a stop to it. I think this is one of the reasons she decided to retire to Rougemont and bring her niece with her. Far from temptation."

Lucille growled and said something in French as she left. Father Lamont sighed as the door closed behind her. "As Lucille said that was not the end of it. We discovered later that the lover simply followed Lisette. He did not come to Rougemont – we have you see, only one tavern here! But he went to a neighbouring town, Valabre. There he took some lodgings and as far as we know continued with his gambling and drinking."

The Earl was listening intently. "You said there were reasons you did not inform me of Felice's death," he reminded the priest. "'Anomalies' you called them. What were they?"

"Monsieur, Felice was a very private person. We knew that she had a guardian in England and a fiancé in India – but that was all. We did not know the names of these people or where they lived exactly and – it is not our custom to pry. We heard that her guardian died in February and that she was very sad, but she did not seem to want to speak about it to anyone. When the avalanche struck, there was so much

134

confusion and grief with so many injured – you can imagine. It was a while before we could think of who we needed to contact on her behalf and by then – Lisette was in control."

The Earl turned sharply from the window. "What do you mean?"

Father Lamont looked uncomfortable. "I mean, Monsieur, Lisette was nursing her in the new house she had taken and was dealing with all correspondence. You may say we were negligent in this matter, having some knowledge of Lisette's character but – Monsieur, she seemed to take her charge so seriously. She seemed a reformed character and besides, there were so many families to look after, so much to do. Even yet we have not even cleared the debris from that night and now the new snows are upon us. It seemed as well to leave Felice to the care of Lisette. Then sadly Felice died. And within hours, Lisette had simply disappeared."

"Disappeared?" echoed the Earl. Jacina glanced at him. His face was drawn and grim.

The priest nodded. "We did not know what to do. We searched Felice's room for correspondence that might tell us how to contact her fiancé in India but – we found nothing." "Nothing?" The Earl looked perplexed. "But she received many letters from my brother, my grandfather and myself. She wrote to me once that she kept them all. The executor of my grandfather's will wrote her at least two letters this year – "

"Monsieur, we found only a letter that Felice had written, not received. It was folded in her bible, but she had not got as far as writing out an envelope so, it was of little use to us. The person she was addressing was a – Hugo. Is that you, Monsieur?"

The Earl nodded. Father Lamont rose and went to a desk where he opened a drawer and took out a folded sheet of paper. He handed it to the Earl who opened it and read it

135

through. A strange look crossed his face. He glanced at Jacina and then put the letter in his waistcoat pocket.

"Thank you for safeguarding this letter," he said in a low voice. "But I do not understand why you found no others."

Father Lamont sighed. "The night Felice died, an old woman went to lay her out. This old woman said Lisette came to Felice's room and took away a large bronze box. We came to the conclusion this box held the personal belongings of Mademoiselle Felice. Not only did we find no letters, we found no other personal effects. Jewellery and such things. Everything belonging to Felice, except her clothes, had gone with Lisette."

The Earl's face set grimly. "And where is Lisette now?"

The priest shook his head. "We do not know, Monsieur. She vanished that night. All we know for certain is that she was glimpsed two days later in Valabre with her lover. They hired some horses there. After that, the trail goes cold."

The Earl lifted his head and stared bleakly at the priest. "And the lover? What was the name of this lover?" he asked in a low voice.

Both the Earl and Jacina paled as the priest replied.

"Fronard, Monsieur. His name was Philippe Fronard."

CHAPTER TEN

The Earl arranged for the upkeep of the graves of both Felice and Madame Gravalt. He ordered fresh flowers to be placed there every day. Then he and Jacina took their leave of Father Lamont.

The Earl had chosen not to tell the old priest of his belief that Lisette had come to Castle Ruven in the guise of Felice Delisle. He felt Father Lamont had burdens of care enough.

The Earl seemed lost in thought. He walked swiftly and Jacina hurried to keep pace with him.

A tavern was open on the square. The Earl took Jacina's elbow and guided her towards it. The door opened into a fug of warmth and pleasant odours. The Earl sat Jacina down at a table by the tiny latticed window. He ordered hot milk for Jacina and a brandy for himself. Then he took out the letter from Felice that the priest had given him earlier. He handed it to Jacina and she looked questioningly at him.

"Read it," he said. His eyes gave nothing away.

Jacina saw that the letter was dated March 24th 1857. The day before the avalanche!

Dear Hugo, she read,

I know you are honouring both the memory of your grand-father and your brother in pursuing marriage with me and indeed I have been a willing accomplice in this. I believed that you might come to replace my beloved Crispian and that in time I would forget him. Now that I have recovered fully from my illness and am here in this peaceful place I have had time to reconsider. The truth is I have come to believe I could not make you a good wife. I do not believe I could be happy so far away from this country. It is after all the country where Crispian and I met. It was amid these mountains that we fell in love and it is amid these mountains that I have now found a measure of serenity. I wish to remain here and train to be a teacher under the guidance of my kind friend, Madame Gravalt.

I hereby release you from any obligation you may believe you owe me.

Your affectionate friend, Felice Delisle.

Jacina's eyes rose slowly from the page.

"You have read it?" the Earl asked gruffly.

"Y..yes, my Lord. I cannot help but believe that...Felice has now found peace and tranquillity...buried here amidst her beloved mountains."

The Earl nodded. "Let us hope so." He took the letter from her and put it back in his waistcoat pocket. For a moment he and Jacina sat in silence, Jacina with her eyes cast down. Finally the Earl spoke.

"Had things run their natural course and this letter had been sent – I should have been a free man when I arrived back at Castle Ruven."

"Yes, m..my Lord."

"But for now I am still yoked."

Jacina looked up and caught the Earl's gaze. She thought she saw a yearning expression in his eyes, but if she did it was quickly stifled. He gave her in its place a bitter smile.

"Still yoked," he repeated, "until I have brought that fiendish pair to justice."

He drained his glass and rose from the table.

"It is noon," he said. "We must leave for Savrin at once."

This time the Earl placed Jacina behind him in the saddle. His body shielded her from the cold wind that arose as they left Rougemont. It began to snow lightly and the village was soon lost in a white, fluttering veil.

The sky overhead that had seemed so bright and unsullied that morning now loomed heavily. It was swollen with snow. The Earl urged the horse on anxiously. He feared a blizzard, though he said nothing to Jacina.

In their separate minds they were each adjusting to the pieces of the same, strange puzzle.

It was clear that Lisette knew all about the fortunes of Felice Delisle. What she did not know before the avalanche she learned afterwards, for she was at liberty to read every single letter Felice had ever received, while Felice herself lay in a helpless coma. She knew that Felice was to make an excellent marriage to a man she had never met. She knew the old Earl had bequeathed a generous sum to Felice should her husband die without issue. She even knew what Felice never knew – that Hugo Earl of Ruven had been wounded at the siege of Delhi and was blind. The letter with this information had arrived in June, while Felice lay in a coma. The news must have later seemed particularly fortuitous, for who knew what accurate description of his fiancée, Crispian had written to his brother out in India?

When Felice died, Lisette knew everything she needed to know in order to step into the dead girl's shoes. Once she was married to the Earl, she only had to arrange an 'accident' to her husband and she was in possession of a title and a large sum of money – not to mention the Ruven diamonds and other jewels that she had been given.

Jacina shivered as a cold blast of wind roared through the ravine ahead and beset the travellers with a wild flurry of snow.

Lisette and Fronard could not deny their evil machinations. The Earl had a village full of witnesses as to their true identity.

Suppose however the Earl should die before he managed to unmask them publicly?

With this new thought Jacina felt fear run through her veins like icy water. She regretted now that the Earl had not told Father Lamont the full story. If Fronard and Lisette believed the story was already public, they would not dare to do anything to the Earl. If however, only the Earl knew, then killing him was as urgent a matter as ever.

Jacina did not for a moment consider her own position. All her fears were for the Earl.

The Earl urged the horse on. It bent its head low against the gathering wind.

The travellers entered the ravine. Jacina rested her forehead against the Earl's back. She was comforted by the warmth she felt through his great coat. Despite her rising fear, despite the bitter cold, she was almost happy. Her body swayed with his to the undulating motion of the horse's flanks.

When the wind died down for a moment the ravine was as silent and icy as a tomb. The only sound came when one of the horse's hooves struck a stone that jutted above the snow line.

Their progress was slow. The sky seemed to press down on them. As suddenly as it had ceased, the wind started up again. It came screaming down the canyon carrying a blinding mass of snow.

They rode out from the ravine into a full blown blizzard.

The road to Savrin was buried in snow. The blizzard whirled and shrieked about them. The horse baulked at the force being hurled against him. He could barely move forward. The Earl dismounted and took the reins.

He would have to lead the horse and Jacina the twenty miles to Savrin. Then, through the icy mass in the air, the shape of a coach loomed.

The Earl turned his face up to Jacina. "We are saved," he breathed.

The coach-driver who had brought them from St Moritz to Savrin and then on to the ravine, must have anticipated their difficulties.

The Earl helped Jacina from the horse as the coach drew up a few feet away.

The coach driver was heavily muffled in a cloak and scarf. A hat was pulled low over his forehead. Only his eyes were visible. He gave no sign of greeting and some instinct made the Earl suddenly quite still, moving neither his head nor his eyes.

The window of the coach was rolled down and a gloved hand appeared, beckoning.

Jacina turned questioningly to the Earl. She was startled at his apparently unseeing gaze and slowly looked back at the coachman. Were the coachman and companion bandits? Was the Earl playing for time?

The hand at the carriage window still beckoned. The coachman jerked his head at Jacina.

"You, Mademoiselle!" he shouted. "You're wanted."

Jacina hesitated.

"You – Monsieur – tell her to approach the carriage."

"I will not," said the Earl.

"What's that?" The coachman raised his whip and it lashed through the air. The Earl recoiled and put a hand to his face. Jacina gasped as she saw a thin line of blood appear on his cheek. The coachman raised his whip again but Jacina cried out.

"That's enough. I..I'm going."

"No, Jacina!" cried the Earl, but she was already moving towards the coach. In a second she was at the carriage window. The gloved hand opened the carriage door and a low voice whispered, "why don't you get in out of ze cold?"

Jacina reeled. A rush of scent reached her from the depths of the carriage, sickly sweet as funeral lilies. In her shock she could not help but cry out. "M..my Lord!"

The Earl made a move towards her, but was stopped in his tracks by the report of a gun. The sound shattered through even the hiss of the wind and the snow. The packhorse reared on its hind legs, then turned and fled back into the ravine. Jacina stared after it in despair.

"Move another inch," cried the voice from within the carriage, "and your little helper here dies."

The gloved hand was pointing a pistol directly at Jacina.

The Earl was unable to hide the contempt in his voice as he replied. "A shot from one of my own pistols, I presume?"

Lisette Gravalt leaned from the carriage window and looked up at the coachman.

"Mon cher," she called, "did you steal a pistol from zis gentleman's castle?"

"Ma chère, I did," replied Fronard mockingly. "Such a pretty one with a pearl handle."

"You are a blackguard, sir!" cried the Earl.

"It is you who are the blackguard, Monsieur," snapped Lisette. "Last night you had a date with me but you did not keep it. This morning we went to ze hotel to find out why. Ze concierge tells us that you had a little visitor yesterday and that today you had gone in a coach together. I did not need to ask where. Rougemont, I thought. And now I find you in ze company of this – what is she in those ridiculous clothes? An old gypsy woman? You would jilt your wife for this creature? Oh, but of course – you cannot see how laide – how ugly she looks!"

"I do not doubt," said the Earl recklessly, "that whatever she is wearing she has more grace, more beauty in her little finger than you have, Madam, in your whole body."

Jacina raised her eyes in wonder to the Earl.

Lisette's voice blazed. "Ha! Fronard! Do you hear this fool?"

"I do," sneered Fronard. "Tell him I will take great pleasure in spoiling that grace, that beauty, when the time comes – "

"What do you mean, sir?" cried the Earl.

Lisette had collected herself. "Enough about this Mademoiselle Nobody. Jaceeeeeena! Just tell us, Monsieur. What did you find out about us from ze helpful citizens of my little village?"

"I found out," said the Earl through gritted teeth, "that

you are as dastardly a pair of villains as ever walked the earth."

Lisette regarded him with steely eyes. "Zat is a pity, Monsieur. Because now I must definitely kill you and your little friend. What a poor, grieving widow I will be, with nothing but a title and money to console me."

"If I am found with a bullet in the head," said the Earl quickly, "there will be no money. I would not have died, I would have been murdered. Until it was discovered by whom, the will could not be executed."

Lisette and Fronard exchanged a glance.

"The authorities will think it is bandits," said Fronard. "The mountains are full of them."

"It is still murder," said the Earl. "As the beneficiary of the will, Madam, you would still be investigated. The authorities – would pay their own visit to Rougemont."

Jacina listened with mounting terror. She knew the Earl was fighting now for her life and his own, but she could imagine no way out of this dilemma.

Lisette regarded the Earl with a worried frown, biting her lip all the while. Now suddenly she reached out and prodded Jacina with the pistol. "You. Get in."

Jacina cast a wild look at the Earl. She did not want to be parted from him. Their destiny now, terrible as it might be, was surely together. "My...my Lord"

"Get in, Jacina," said the Earl firmly.

Still Jacina hesitated, her heart thumping in her breast. Then she felt cold fingers sink themselves into her hair. She gave a cry as she was yanked brutally backwards and flung onto the carriage floor.

"Do not harm her!" cried the Earl. He lunged for the coach but the whip came whistling from above. It cut across his brow and he staggered back. Jacina gave a cry and tried to rise but Lisette pushed her down. Then Lisette leaned from the carriage window and laughed at the Earl.

"I am not going to shoot you after all, dear husband," she said. "I am just going to leave you here. No-one will travel in zis blizzard. Your horse is gone and you cannot see. Night is coming on. You will freeze to death – or fall over ze edge of ze mountain and it will not look like murder. There will be no investigation."

"And – Jacina?" asked the Earl in a low voice.

"Oh, we cannot leave her here with you. She has eyes, Monsieur. She could help you survive. No, no, she must come with us. We will find another way of – dealing with her. Au revoir, mon cher!"

Fronard cracked the whip and they were on their way. Jacina struggled up to gaze from the window. The figure of the Earl stood like stone in the swirling snow. Then he was gone.

She sank miserably onto the seat opposite Lisette Gravalt. Her back hurt where she had fallen on the carriage floor. Loose strands of hair hung about her face. Her mind was feverish as she tried to think of how she might help the Earl.

Lisette was watching her, the pistol still in her hand.

"What a pleasure to be alone together," she smirked.

"Believe me, the pleasure is all yours," said Jacina stiffly.

Lisette gave a shriek of laughter. For the first time Jacina wondered if she was not perhaps a little mad.

"You don't like my company? It is not good enough for you? That is what they were always thinking. At ze school in Geneva. All ze pupils were 'Mademoiselle' this, 'Mademoiselle' that. I was only ever 'Lisette'. 'Lisette, bring ze tea. Lisette, clean ze blackboard'."

Jacina brushed a strand of hair back. She was thinking quickly. If she kept Lisette talking...if she managed to distract her...perhaps she could wrest the pistol out of her hands.

"I am sure it was not as bad as all that," she said.

"Ha!" cried Lisette. "You think not? I will tell you!"

She was fourteen when her aunt took her into the school. The other pupils were from privileged backgrounds and were indulged, yes, indulged by Madame Gravalt while she, Madame's niece, was expected to fetch and carry. While the other girls prepared for wealthy marriages, she had to prepare to be a dull old teacher, like her aunt. This was unfair. She was the most beautiful girl in the school, everybody thought so. She was clever, too. She watched the other girls and learned how to walk, how to speak, how to behave like a lady of class. She listened to the pupils from England and learned how to speak English.

Whatever she did, though, she could not please her aunt. Her aunt told her she was vain and ambitious and it would do her no good to have ideas above her station.

"But who is ze Countess now?" cried Lisette triumphantly. "Who has ze diamonds now?"

Of all the girls in the school it was Felice whom Lisette resented most. Felice was the star pupil. She was so *good* it made Lisette sick. Madame Gravalt loved Felice more than she did her own niece. She encouraged Felice's romance with Crispian Ruven, but when Lisette herself fell in love, with Fronard, her aunt forbade her to see him.

"And my lover is a man," said Lisette scornfully. "Not a pale, skinny boy like Crispian!"

Listening intently, Jacina was thrown sideways as the coach gave a lurch. She was sitting with her back to the coach driver's box and she could hear Fronard cursing and beating the horses. The creatures were struggling valiantly, but the wind was fierce and the blizzard was like icy needles in their flesh. The coach was moving in a cumbrous fashion.

Lisette did not seem to notice. Her eyes glittered as she continued her tale.

When Felice's fiancé died and Felice became ill and went away to a sanatorium, Lisette was glad to be rid of her. She did not even mind when her aunt took her to Rougemont to live. There were no other girls for her aunt to continually compare her with and her workload was less. Her lover came to a nearby town to be near her and she was often able to sneak out and see him. She was sure her aunt would eventually come round to the idea of her and Fronard marrying. Then Felice recovered from her illness and came to live with Madame Gravalt in Rougemont. Lisette was incensed. Not only was Felice back to absorb all Madame Gravalt's attention, she had meanwhile acquired another rich and titled fiancé.

"But then at last ze Gods were with me!"

"W..what do you mean?" asked Jacina.

Lisette's eyes burned like torches. *"What flies without wings, hits without hands, and sees without eyes?"*

"I am sure I...do not know."

"The White Death," cried Lisette. "The avalanche! It was sent so that I could at last find a way out of these mountains and this little, little life!"

Jacina heart grew chill at these words and she shivered.

"Oh," said Lisette haughtily, "you are cold are you, with your thin passionless blood? Here!" She drew a small flask from her purse and threw it across the carriage.

It was brandy. Jacina sipped gratefully, eyeing Lisette as she did so. Was this the moment? As she handed the flask back, could she grasp at the pistol? With this intent in mind, she half rose from her seat but Lisette was too quick.

"Oh no. Just throw it on the seat beside me."

The pistol was levelled directly at Jacina's brow. Jacina did as she was instructed.

"You think I am stupid, hein?" Lisette asked with amusement.

Jacina shrugged. She had no intention of replying, but at that moment her eye caught movement on the road behind. She vaguely discerned the shape of a horse and rider through the driving snow. Her heart gave a lurch. Who else could it be in this isolated area but the Earl? His horse had not gone far into the ravine – or had returned of its own accord – and he was now in pursuit of the coach. He had managed to catch up with them because the coach was moving so slowly.

She looked back at Lisette. She must keep her kidnapper's attention occupied.

"No," she said slowly. "I do not think you are stupid. I think you are very, very clever. Reading all those letters while Felice was in a coma...gathering all the information...playing your part so wonderfully in Castle Ruven. Who could have guessed that you were not Felice herself?"

Lisette's eyes gleamed with malice. "Only you," she said. "Only you suspected something. But for your meddling, our plan would have gone so smoothly. And for that, you are going to pay with your life."

At that moment there was a thump on the roof of the coach. Lisette's head jerked up. "What was that?"

"A s..stone, I'm sure," said Jacina. From the window she could see the horse falling riderless behind. The Earl was on the coach!

Lisette's eyes narrowed. She was uncertain. Then

there came the sound of a struggle from the coachman's box. The coach began to lurch wildly from side to side. Lisette rushed to the window and leaned out, twisting her body round so that she could point the pistol at the box. Jacina saw the pistol waver as it followed the movement of the figures fighting above. She must seize her chance. She leaped up and seized Lisette's arm, trying to drag it back in through the window. With her free hand Lisette attempted to hold her at arm's length. They struggled for a moment and then a shot rang out, reverberating from peak to peak. There was a groan and a body fell through the air, landing with a soft thud into the thick snow.

It was Fronard.

Lisette dropped the pistol and gave a wild shriek, like an animal pierced by an arrow. She flung herself from the still moving coach, and ran to his body.

"He is dead, he is dead," she screamed. "I have killed him!"

The coach lurched to a halt and the Earl jumped down. He scooped up the pistol and moved swiftly over to Lisette and the prone Fronard.

Jacina was shaking as she climbed from the carriage. She waited shivering by the carriage door.

Lisette was covering Fronard's face with kisses. The Earl put a hand on her shoulder.

"Come Madam," he said. "There is nothing you can do here."

Lisette wrenched herself free and staggered to her feet, staring at him in bewilderment. "You – you can see!"

"Yes, Madam, I can see."

Lisette threw her head back with a loud moan. The Earl put out his hand.

149

"Let me lead you to the coach," he said.

"No, no!" Lisette stared wildly around like an animal trying to find a way out of a trap.

The Earl insisted. "Madam, you must."

"To go where?" cried Lisette. "To prison? To a life without my Phillipe? No, never. Never." She began to edge away from the Earl.

"Look out – take care!" warned the Earl with a frown.

Lisette did not heed him. She turned and stumbled into the blinding snow. There was a rattle of loose rocks – a plunging scream – and Lisette was gone.

A deep, icy chasm had claimed her forever.

Jacina covered her face with her hands. She heard footfalls in the snow as the Earl came to her. She felt his strong, tender arms clasp her safely to his manly chest.

"My darling, oh my darling!" he whispered. "I have yearned for you for so long. Even before the woman I thought was my fiancée came to Castle Ruven – your voice melted my heart. I tried so hard to remain strong in the face of duty. I made myself cold towards you when you so innocently offended Felice. I made myself doubt your words, when you told me what you had seen in the garden. But now, at last, I may claim you! Tell me that is your wish. Tell me that you have longed for me as I have longed for you!"

"Oh, y..yes, Hugo...I have," breathed Jacina.

"Then you are mine!" cried the Earl. "Body and soul – you are mine!"

"I love you...I love you...I love you...Hugo..."

He held her even tighter and looked adoringly into her eyes. "I now realise that I must have loved you from the moment I rescued the best bonnet from the stream and gave it back to a tiny enchantress with golden hair and green eyes.

You have been my ideal for all these years and now I can declare my eternal love for you."

His lips sought hers. The blizzard raged about them, the wind howled, but they were lost in their mutual embrace. The heat of passion burned in their veins.

At last the Earl pulled away with a long sigh. Gazing deep into Jacina's eyes, he traced a finger gently across her cheek. "Sweetheart, let us drive on to Savrin. We will return to England, to our friends at Castle Ruven. There we will be married. And this time, my darling, it will be a marriage made in heaven, with both our hearts entwined and we will make it last forever."

Jacina felt herself melt, softer and more yielding than the snow itself....